RACING AHEAD OF TIME

"Well, QL47, what happens next?" Jeanette asked. "How do we go about helping the aliens?"

"That's hard to say."

"You mean you don't know!"

The robot shook his head. "I only know that without intervention, they will all die."

Jeanette closed her eyes, thinking of Amy. She was scared for all of them, but Amy was someone she knew and cared about. "We have to do something."

"We thought for sure you'd know what we needed to do, QL47," Jesse added quietly. "Seems to me we could do more damage than good by racing ahead to try to help."

"That is possible." QL47 nodded again. "That is, of course, the great risk of time intervention. . . ."

BOOK 3 OF THE TIME KEEPER

WHEN DREAMERS CEASE TO DREAM

BARBARA BARTHOLOMEW

A SIGNET VISTA BOOK

NEW AMERICAN LIBRARY

PUBLISHER'S NOTE

This novel is a work of fiction. Names, characters, places, and incidents either are the product of the author's imagination or are used fictitiously, and any resemblance to actual persons, living or dead, events, or locales is entirely coincidental.

NAL BOOKS ARE AVAILABLE AT QUANTITY DISCOUNTS
WHEN USED TO PROMOTE PRODUCTS OR SERVICES.
FOR INFORMATION PLEASE WRITE TO PREMIUM MARKETING DIVISION,
NEW AMERICAN LIBRARY, 1633 BROADWAY,
NEW YORK, NEW YORK 10019.

RL 6/IL 5+

SIGNET VISTA TRADEMARK REG. U.S. PAT. OFF. AND FOREIGN COUNTRIES
REGISTERED TRADEMARK—MARCA REGISTRADA
HECHO EN CHICAGO, U.S.A.

SIGNET, SIGNET CLASSIC, MENTOR, PLUME, MERIDIAN AND NAL BOOKS
are published by New American Library,
1633 Broadway, New York, New York 10019

First Printing, October, 1985

1 2 3 4 5 6 7 8 9

PRINTED IN THE UNITED STATES OF AMERICA

FOR DONNA IVY

CHAPTER ONE

Jeanette stared unhappily at what was left of the birthday cake her stepmother had made and listened to her dad's side of the argument, taking place over the telephone.

"I'd like another piece of cake," her brother Neil said. Nobody answered or even seemed to hear. He helped himself to a large slice of the chocolate layer cake. "Happy birthday." Neil smiled at Jeanette.

She smiled back. "Some birthday," she whispered.

He nodded, then bent closer. "Thought of a plan yet?"

She shook her head. How could she think of anything with all this going on? She tuned back in to the phone conversation Dad was carrying on with Mom. Considering what rates must be from France to Texas, it had to be costing Mom a bundle to yell at her former husband.

Jeanette grinned. Knowing Mom, she probably considered every penny well spent.

"It isn't funny, Jeanette," her stepmother scolded.

"No, Lillian, it isn't," Jeanette agreed fervently. "It sure isn't. Like Neil just said, this is some birthday."

Lillian Lacy sat down in the chair next to her, smoothing her skirts gracefully. "It certainly isn't what your father and I had planned for you."

Usually Jeanette resented anything that even sounded like criticism of her mother, but this afternoon she couldn't help agreeing. If Mom hadn't interfered, she would at this moment be the proud owner of a new car, the gift of her father and stepmother on her sixteenth birthday. Keli, her stepsister, already had an automobile of her own. But Mom had refused to allow them to "spoil" Jeanette. It wasn't fair! Jeanette couldn't help feeling bitter, but she knew she'd feel even worse at this moment if she didn't have a much more serious problem to occupy her mind.

She couldn't help thinking about Jesse, spending this dreary winter day over at the abandoned apartment where Amy and Selma used to live. They had to come up with a plan—and quickly. None of them could stand this waiting much longer.

"I'm sorry you feel that way, Cara."

She tried to pay attention to her father's phone conversation.

"Of course, we'll abide by your wishes, but it's hardly our fault if Jeanette blames you for depriving her of something she wanted very much."

Apparently his former wife let him have it because he moved the receiver away from his ear a little. An angry Cara Lacy was a formidable woman: small, dark, and fiery. Jeanette just bet her mother was giving it to Dad with both barrels.

He was not, however, a man to be intimidated; he stood his ground calmly. "I believe we've said all there is to say on the subject, Cara. Would you like to say goodbye to your daughter now?"

Still angry about the car, Jeanette didn't want to say anything to her mother, but when she didn't move from her chair, Dad frowned and motioned to her. She got up and went over reluctantly to take the receiver. "Hi, Mom."

"Don't speak to me in that tone of voice, Jeanette Lacy." The angry crackle was still in her mother's voice.

"Sorry."

"I just wanted to wish you happy birthday before I hung up." The tone softened considerably. "You don't know how much I wanted to be there with you."

"We just saw each other at Christmas." To her embarrassment, Jeanette found her voice cracking with emotion. Why was it that no matter how old she got, she still missed her mother at special occasions and couldn't help thinking of the old days before the divorce when they would have all been together? It was about time she adjusted to reality. She cleared her throat, determined to sound normal. "Anyway, that was a great present you sent. I can't wait to tell Tina that I've got clothes from Paris."

Her mother laughed. "They aren't exactly designer originals, baby."

"Just the fact that they come from Paris will be enough to impress Tina."

"Well, I'm glad you liked them. Be talking to you soon. Give Neil a hug for me."

Jeanette looked doubtfully to where her twelve-year-old brother was still eating chocolate cake. "Will it be okay if I just tell him you miss him?"

Her mother laughed again. "Bye, Jeanette."

"Goodbye." Jeanette hung up and turned to find Dad sitting stiffly at the table, Lillian at his side looking worriedly at him. She sighed, hoping she wasn't going to catch it from Lillian at the first private moment for upsetting Dad again. Her stepmother tended to be a little overprotective where her husband was concerned.

Jeanette wished she could escape up to the room she shared with Keli, but she could hardly leave her own birthday celebration, even if it was only a family party.

"You haven't finished opening your presents yet," Dad said, deliberately trying to lighten things up again after the disastrous phone argument.

Somehow presents didn't seem that exciting when you were sixteen and had been hoping in spite of everything for a car of your own, but Jeanette tried to look pleased as she moved down to the end of the table where the gifts were piled. If only she had a car of her own, then she could go see Jesse without so much hassle. "Only this one big one left unopened," she announced, falsely cheerful. She picked up the package and shook it. "Now who can this be from?"

"You know it's from Dad and Lillian," Neil said scornfully. "You practically picked it out."

Lillian looked guilty. "We didn't want to choose something she wouldn't like."

"I'm sure I'll love it," Jeanette said hurriedly. Cara Lacy, her mom, delighted in surprises and would never have allowed her daughter to pick out her own present—even if the gift misfired and was the last thing Jeanette wanted.

"Well, open it," Neil grumbled, "so we can see what you got."

With an air of drama, Jeanette tore ribbons and ripped paper. Finally she pulled out the cassette player she'd chosen for herself from the newspaper ad Lillian had shown her. "Just what I wanted," she exclaimed with mock surprise.

"You've ruined the bow." Lillian looked mournfully at the shredded wrappings.

"One more package." Neil pointed to a small one that had been hidden behind the gift from her parents.

She picked it up. "No card," she said, frowning. Without a show this time, she opened it to find a small jewelry box. When she lifted the top, she couldn't help but gasp at the sight of what lay inside. It was a tiny silver unicorn on a delicate matching chain. She stared at it for a minute, than fastened it around her neck.

"How lovely," Lillian exclaimed. "So dainty. It's exquisitely made."

"Who is it from?" Keli asked curiously.

Jeanette shook her head. "There wasn't any card." Who else but Jesse would send her a unicorn necklace?

"Did you get it for your sister, Neil?" Dad asked, frowning.

Neil shook his head. "I got her the box of chocolates."

"Oh, yes." Dad nodded. "A box of your favorite chocolates." He eyed his only son with disfavor.

"But who could have sent this present?" Lillian looked around as though suspecting someone of playing a trick. "None of us got it."

Suddenly Keli giggled, sounding younger than her sixteen years. "I'll bet it's from a secret admirer."

Jeanette eyed her stepsister without animosity, for once not even jealous of the dark blue eyes and long black hair that made Keli so stunning. Well, not very jealous, she amended. After all, she was human! "You're the one with secret admirers, Keli."

She was grateful when the ringing of the doorbell attracted attention away from her. Taking advantage of the moment, she whispered to Neil, "Don't suppose you know how that got here?"

He shrugged, trying to look innocent. "Guess somebody must have dropped it by when we weren't looking."

"Sure!"

"He wanted to surprise you so he asked me to slip it in with your other things."

"How did he seem?"

"Kind of down. He'd like to get into action."

"So would we all." Jeanette nodded. "These last two days have been miserable."

"Then why don't we just get going?"

"It isn't that simple and you know it. We can't help Amy or QL47 or anyone if we go dashing in and get ourselves captured."

"I've been trying to think of a wonderful idea," he admitted, wrinkling his forehead to show how hard he'd been concentrating. "And I feel sure I'm just on the edge of something."

Jeanette couldn't help laughing even though he looked hurt. "We need all the brain power we've got." She tried to sound serious.

Keli, who'd gone to answer the door, came back with a tall man who looked vaguely familiar to Jeanette. "This is my mom and dad, Mr. Calloway," Keli said in introduction.

Jeanette's first reaction was irritation at Keli calling her father "Dad." After all, Keli had a perfectly good father of her own living in another state. And Jeanette didn't call Lillian "Mom." Then the words penetrated. Mr. Calloway! She'd seen him around school. That was it, he was one of the new assistant principals.

Keli indicated her. "And this is my sister, Jeanette, Mr. Calloway."

"Glad to meet you, Jeanette."

She nodded, almost entirely certain she wasn't glad to meet him. What was going on now?

Surely they hadn't somehow found out about Jesse?

"Is there some problem, Mr. Calloway?" Ron Lacy waved the other man to a seat. "Neither Keli or Jeanette have said anything, but of course if something's wrong we want to know about it."

"Oh, I'm sure it's not Keli," Lillian blurted out, then her face reddened. "We have confidence in both our girls," she added quickly.

"No trouble," Mr. Calloway assured them, his manner relaxed and comfortable. "At least not in the way you mean. Thing is, Mr. Lacy, I've been put in charge of attendance problems at Northeast High. We have some chronic absentees that we're anxious to get back into school."

"I can understand that." Dad nodded.

"We've been going over our records, checking things out on the computer, and something odd turned up."

"What's that?" Dad was trying to be patient, Jeanette knew, but like her he was beginning to wonder what the point of this visit was.

"We check on our students when they're absent. Someone calls the home and confirms that the parents are aware the student isn't in school and learns what the problem is."

Ron Lacy nodded. "When Neil and Jeanette were . . . away . . . last fall, someone called each day. I can appreciate the effort."

Jeanette couldn't help wishing Dad hadn't reminded the assistant principal of her own absences. That little outing last fall when Neil had been missing and she'd had to go looking for him had cost her four unexcused absences, and the office staff had reminded her of that fact more than once.

"Well, it so happened that the clerk who checks on sophomore-class absences was making her calls when one of the teachers, a Mrs. Simpson, was in the office."

Jeanette caught her breath. Mrs. Simpson taught geometry.

"It was the first day this student had been absent so the clerk wouldn't have thought much about it when the phone didn't answer. She'd have just figured the girl was sick and her folks took her to the doctor or something like that."

"Or maybe the phone was out of order," Jeanette offered quickly. She was very much afraid she knew where this was headed. She and Amy both were in Mrs. Simpson's geometry class and Amy had been absent today.

"Something like that," Mr. Calloway agreed, glancing at Jeanette a little suspiciously. "As I say, the clerk wouldn't have thought anything about it, but the teacher heard her mention the student's name and came over to ask her about it. Said the girl was in her class and hadn't been there for days."

"But you said she'd only been absent for one day," Lillian corrected gently.

Mr. Calloway leaned back, stretching out his long legs. His manner seemed almost excessively casual. Jeanette was beginning to be uncomfortably aware that he was watching for her reaction.

"That's what's really strange. Our records showed she'd been in school right through Friday, but the teacher insisted she'd been out much longer and that she'd been turning in reports that indicated as much. So we started checking with this girl's other teachers and got the same story. Seems as though once the information was fed into the computer, it corrected itself and reported her as having been present."

Jeanette glanced desperately at Neil, sure he was as aware as she of what was coming. His gaze was questioning and she shook her head slightly. The only thing they could do was pretend ignorance.

"Some of these kids are real sharp with the computers," Mr. Calloway went on, "but the staff members were shocked at the idea that this girl would be involved in anything like that. They say she's a real quiet kid, bright too, never in any trouble, except for that little incident last fall."

"Wait a minute!" Scowling, Dad got to his feet. "If you're trying to say my daughter has been playing hookey . . ."

"No, Dad," Jeanette corrected quietly. "I don't think he's talking about me." She and Neil hadn't been the only ones absent last fall. Amy had waited for them beside the steps in the cavern, waited for them to come back from traveling in time. "It's about Amy, isn't it?"

He nodded.

"I knew she'd been missing some school. We have a couple of classes together."

"But my daughter had no way of knowing there'd been any hanky-panky with the computer," Ron Lacy protested.

"Of course not," his wife agreed. "And we've all known that Amy's been unwell. Jeanette's been very concerned about her."

"I'm sure you've just had a misfunction in your software or something like that," Jeanette's dad said. "Amy is my daughter's best friend and certainly not the kind of person who would do anything underhanded."

Jeanette wished she could tell Dad that it wasn't that Amy had wanted to do anything deceitful. She'd simply been desperate to be left alone after Selma died. But Dad didn't even know about Selma. Amy wouldn't let them tell anyone.

The assistant principal shook his head. "I'm afraid it isn't quite that simple. You've got to understand, Mr. Lacy, this has gone beyond a routine inquiry about a little misbehavior. We're seriously concerned about Amy Cornell."

"That's easily resolved. We'll get in my car and go over to her apartment right now. My daughter can show you where she lives."

Mr. Calloway didn't budge. "We've already done that."

Jeanette felt as though her heart dropped to the bottom of her stomach. Jesse was staying at Amy's abandoned apartment. Had he been discovered?

"Nobody was there, Mr. Lacy. Not the girl or her family. Funny part was we found no evidence of that family. Looked as if she lived there alone, though the office clerks insisted they'd talked to an aunt or some other relative last fall when the girl was missing. Anyhow, she didn't seem to have taken much in the way of clothes or luggage or anything. Everything seemed to be in place as best we could tell. It's as though she just upped and vanished."

It was as good a description as any, Jeanette thought, but she could hardly tell Mr. Calloway that her friend was in actual fact an alien being come to earth in the distant future, who had traveled back in time as an infant to come here to live, and that now she'd gone ahead to join her own people. No! No way was she going to tell Mr. Calloway or anyone else that story. Who would believe her?

"At this point we were really getting worried, especially when a clerk at the office remembered that someone had made inquiries about the girl. She remembered that it was the mother of another student, a Tina Parker."

"Why Tina is another of Jeanette's friends," Lillian said.

Mr. Calloway nodded. "We talked to the Parkers and they said the girl was at their place Saturday afternoon. They'd found her sick and alone and took her into their home, but Saturday night she left. They thought she'd come here."

"Here?" Lillian looked puzzled. "But we haven't seen Amy in ages. Why would they think she was here?"

"Because of the friendship with your daughter. In fact, Tina was a little annoyed because she thought the two girls were playing tricks on her."

"That's ridiculous. We would have been happy

to take in Jeanette's friend if we'd known anything about this. But we hadn't an inkling."

"Jeanette?" Mr. Calloway was looking in her direction and Jeanette tried not to squirm.

"Tina called me to say Amy was sick and staying at her house. That's the last I heard."

Dad was still standing. Mr. Calloway stood up. His relaxed, easygoing manner dropped. "We want you to understand how serious this is, Jeanette. If you have any knowledge of the whereabouts of Amy Cornell, this is the time to tell us before public announcements are made and the police alerted."

"The police?"

"Jeanette doesn't know anything," Neil interrupted, his tone so decisive as to be almost rude. "She already told you that."

"Neil!" his stepmother scolded.

"Well, she doesn't."

Jeanette knew what he was doing. He was trying to give her time to recover before she had to talk. He knew as well as she where Amy was right now and that she was in real danger. But the situation wasn't one with which the Dallas police or the staff at Northeast High School could help.

She drew in a deep breath, tried to steady her voice. "If I hear from Amy, I'll be sure and let you know."

The phone rang suddenly, startlingly loud. Mr. Calloway looked at her as though he was trying to read her expression.

"Answer that in the kitchen, Neil," Dad instructed. "We don't want to be interrupted right now." He turned again to the visitor. "I can assure you, Mr. Calloway, that we're all fond of Amy and anxious to know that she's safe."

"I'm sure." Jeanette had a feeling Mr. Calloway was convinced that she could lead him to Amy. Well, in a way it was true, but nobody would be more shocked than the assistant principal if she did that very thing.

Neil came back into the room. "That was a friend of yours," he told Jeanette.

"Not Amy." Dad turned to frown at him.

"No, it was Jake. He said to tell you he'd see you real soon."

"Jake?" Jeanette couldn't think of anyone she knew by that name. Oh, there was a Jake or two at school, but no one she really knew. . . .

Neil looked at her as though she were an especially unintelligent form of life on the planet. "Jake," he said again, "the guy who sent you the unicorn necklace for your birthday."

He meant Jesse. Jesse had called and for some reason needed to see her urgently. Jeanette knew her brother wouldn't have gone to the trouble to tell her in front of the others this way unless something important was going on.

"Aha! The secret admirer!" Keli proclaimed.

Nobody seemed interested. They were too worried about Amy.

"I think it might be best if you talked to the police, Jeanette," Mr. Calloway suggested. "Perhaps your parents would like to accompany you downtown."

"Is that really necessary?" Jeanette's dad asked.

"We're going to have Amy's picture shown on

television and in the papers, Mr. Lacy, and any information Jeanette can give the police about her likes and dislikes—you know, where she might head, might be helpful. I'm sure they'll want to question her at length."

Jeanette wanted to object, but there seemed no way out of this. She tried to draw comfort from the knowledge that Amy wasn't going to be bothered by any of this, but she hated to think of all the people who would be looking for her.

"She can't go yet," Neil objected. "She's got to talk to Jake first."

"Really, Neil." Lillian frowned at her stepson. "We'll worry about your sister's little romance later."

"But, Jeanette." Neil ignored the rest of them. "Jake said to tell you he has this great idea he wants to tell you about and he'll meet you at the rocky place."

The rocky place! Neil was really being devious. Jesse was going to meet them out where four stones, all that was left of the timeway they'd discovered under the old hotel, were strung across the backyard.

She was still trying to take it all in, to grasp the garbled message Neil was trying to transmit.

"Jake says to be sure and wear your traveling clothes."

"I don't think Jeanette had better plan on taking any trips right now," Mr. Calloway said firmly. "At least not until her friend is located."

Jeanette gave a slight nod in her brother's direction to show that she got the message, then she smiled at the assistant principal. "Isn't it cold outside, Mr. Calloway?"

"A bit on the chilly side. It's windy."

"Then I'd better get my coat. I'll be right back."

She was pleased to see that Neil, leaving the adults to talk, followed her from the room. "Does Jesse have his coverall?" she whispered as they raced up the stairs toward their bedrooms.

He nodded. "Took it with him. Said he'd be here in a few minutes."

"Then we'll be ready."

Neil's eyebrows slid upward. "We're going to walk on the timeway while it's still light outside? What if someone spots us?"

"We have to take that chance."

She heard Neil's bedroom door slam as she raced into her own room. She ran to the closet and dug out her suitcase. Still packed away in the bottom was a silky yellow coverall and a pair of shiny shoes. Hurriedly she put on the coverall and then sat down to put on the shoes, which seemed to mold themselves against her feet.

She'd just finished dressing when Keli opened the door. "What kind of a strange outfit is that?"

"This?" Jeanette whirled around as though showing it off. "Oh, it's the latest."

"From Paris? That's one of the things your mother sent you? The design is certainly plain, though the fabric is very unusual looking and the shoes—"

"I've got to go. Mr. Calloway is waiting."

"But you forgot your coat!"

Jeanette ignored her stepsister's call and hurried back to the stairs. Neil came out of his room just as she started down. He was wearing a bright red suit that matched her own in design.

"I'm ready," he announced.

She nodded, suddenly too nervous to talk. She could only hope that this wonderful idea of Jesse's, whatever it was, really was a good one. Otherwise, they were in real trouble. She tried to tell herself that she'd always been able to depend on him before.

They tiptoed down the last few steps to the hall. From the dining room, they could hear the sound of Dad's voice. "I'm sure Jeanette will be right down. Keli will see that she doesn't delay."

Jeanette looked at her brother. They started to sneak down the hall toward the kitchen and the back door.

"Jeanette?" She heard Keli's voice. They tiptoed faster.

"Jesse can't possibly have made it all the way from Amy's apartment," she whispered.

"He didn't call from there. He skipped out when they came around looking for her. He called from a booth only a couple of blocks from here."

They opened the back door carefully to keep from making any sound and stepped outside. It must be about five, maybe even a little later. The winter evening was gloomy, a hazy gray that would soon turn into early darkness. The glow from the four stones, all that was left of the timeway, seemed no stronger than it had been two days ago when they last used it.

Suddenly Neil chuckled. "I heard you telling

Lillian that the stones glowed because they mixed some kind of glittery stuff with the plastic when they made them."

She eyed him impatiently. "It was the best story I could come up with. But we don't have time to worry about that now. Where is Jesse?"

"I'm here." A tall boy with dark hair and intelligent brown eyes stepped from the shadows next to the house. He was dressed, as Jeanette knew he would be, in a light blue coverall, but instead of shoes like the ones she and Neil were wearing, he had on his own well-worn boots. Jesse would only compromise so far. His boots were the symbol of his own lost world. They wore the outfits given them last fall when they'd first traveled in time—Neil and Jeanette Lacy having met Jesse Lansden in his own strange, alternative world which seemed like a distorted version of old west Texas—and he going along with them to the future year of 2061 where they'd been held prisoners. And where they now, hoping to save their friend Amy and all her alien race from certain death, must again journey.

"I hear you finally came up with an idea about how we can get into two thousand sixty-one without being captured," Jeanette told him, trying to conceal how glad she was to see him again.

"Finally!" A wide, engaging grin touched his eyes and lit his whole face. "Well, I was only waiting to give you first chance to show your brilliance. Didn't want to be rude."

"Come on, you two," Neil ordered. "We've probably got two minutes before Dad or someone else comes out here looking for us. Tell us your idea, Jesse, so we can get going."

Jesse nodded, looking solemn, and then motioning them back into the shadows, he began to explain.

CHAPTER TWO

"In the first place," Jesse said, "it's not such a great idea. It's just the only one I could come up with."

Jeanette nodded. She couldn't help thinking that in spite of everything, which included taking two dangerous trips in time, the one last fall and the other just two days ago, she couldn't wish that none of it had happened. If Neil hadn't run away and accidentally stumbled onto the purpose of the timeway, they would never have met Jesse. And irritating though he was, she couldn't imagine life without him anymore. "Tell us anyway. We don't expect wonders."

He opened his mouth to speak, then closed it again. He pushed them back against the wall. "Someone's coming," he whispered.

They hid, shadowed by the house itself, while Keli came to open the back door and lean outside. She looked around for a minute, then pulled the door closed. They could hear her call, "No, Mom, they're not out here."

Neil let his breath out in a soft whistle. "That was close."

Jesse nodded. "We have to hurry." He stepped nearer, fearful someone might overhear. "The way I've got it figured, we've got to hit the guardians at the best possible time."

Jeanette closed her eyes, seeing again the world of the guardians in 2061. It was a fearful place where the timeway was constantly watched and time walking itself considered a criminal infraction. Last fall when they'd stumbled into that time, they'd been confined, very nearly on a permanent basis. They'd only barely managed to escape with the help of their tutor, the humanoid robot, QL47. No telling what had happened to him after they left.

"I've been going over and over the details," Jesse went on. "We've got a lot to worry about: iron bars, those giant-sized police of theirs . . ."

Jeanette nodded. She didn't even like to think about falling into the hands of the brown-clad super police, the Protectors Corps of the Guardians. "And the captain," she added to the list, realizing they'd never even known the name of their enemy. But then he probably didn't have a name. He probably had an alpha-numeric identifier like QL47.

"The more I thought about it, the more complicated it seemed," Jesse explained. "I couldn't see any way we could figure out the best time to get there. But then it struck me: we could let the timeway work it out for us."

Jeanette frowned. "What do you mean?"

"Remember what it was like in two thousand ninety-nine when we took Amy to meet her people? The protectors had abandoned their posts and the gates stood open and unguarded."

She nodded. "Sure, but we can hardly arrange an alien landing to distract the guards' attention."

"Nope, but now that we know how to land at the exact time we choose, we can visualize arriving on the timeway in two thousand sixty-one at the best possible moment."

"If there is such a moment," Jeanette said doubtfully.

"I'm hoping your friend QL47 will arrange it."

"So when we get on the timeway we picture arriving with the guards absent from their posts and the gates open?"

He nodded. "That's it."

"That's all." Neil sounded disappointed.

"It's not a bad idea." Jeanette tried to encourage her brother.

"Anyway it's the best we've got and we've got to work with it." Jesse pointed toward the back door where Keli was leaning out, looking for them with a worried expression on her face. When she went away, he led them out into the open, toward the stones at the back of the yard. "Just don't forget," he called to them in a loud whisper, "that you've got to keep in mind that you're headed for two thousand sixty-one. We don't want to end up in different places."

When they reached the stones, he prepared to step on the first stone from the right, the one they now knew would take them one step into the future to the timeway in 2061. Jeanette watched without protest, knowing that Jesse would insist on going into danger first. But this time she was halfway convinced that the last one to go would be at greater risk. With each arrival, the chance that the protectors would be alerted to the presence of intruders was increased.

She watched the tall boy in the light blue coverall shimmer as though light danced throughout his body, then he disappeared from the last steppingstone.

Jeanette gave her brother a little shove. "You're next, Neil, and don't forget to keep a picture in your mind of when you want to arrive."

He moistened his lips nervously. "You're sure this is going to work, Jean. I mean I've never . . ."

She touched his shoulder lightly. This was his first time to try to give coordinates on the timeway. They had only discovered the possibility on the last trip with Amy and Neil hadn't been with them.

"Nothing to feel funny about if you'd rather stay here," she told him. "We'll send a message to you if we need you, the way QL47 warned us about the aliens."

His eyes widened with horror. "No way are you going to cut me out of the action, Jean."

She laughed softly, wishing she could convince him to stay. It would be one less thing to worry about if she knew Neil was safely at home. But she couldn't blame him for refusing to be left behind. "Then just remember what we've told you about visualizing coordinates. And once you get there, be prepared for anything."

He nodded. "I'm really looking forward to seeing QL47 again."

She watched as Neil, his red coverall especially vivid against the dead winter trees and grass, climbed onto the timeway and vanished just the way Jesse had.

Now came her turn. She tried to put the picture in her mind even before she stepped onto the stone. She visualized the timeway corridor the way she'd last seen it, deserted and abandoned, with the great iron gates standing open. But what if such a time had never occurred in the year 2061? What if there was no unguarded moment?

In spite of her efforts, a picture of the way it probably would look, the gates closed and the protectors swarming all over the place, painted itself in her mind. She shook her head as though to fling the image from it. No! She couldn't think that way or most certainly that was what she'd find when she arrived there.

She tried to erase all doubts, picturing the unguarded timeway so firmly that it was almost real. Like a chant she repeated, "It's two thousand sixty-one. It's two thousand sixty-one."

She stepped on the stone, felt the faint familiar tingling of the soles of her feet, more protected now by the shoes from the future than they'd been by her sneakers on that first trip.

"Two thousand sixty-one," she murmured again as she heard, distantly, the rising sound that meant the timeway was going into action.

It was at that moment that she glanced across the yard toward the house. She saw her stepsister standing in the doorway, gazing at her with a look of absolute horror, her mouth moving soundlessly. Keli!

The sound rose to a high-pitched shriek, and a swirling of color enveloped her so that she saw Keli through streaks of waving gold and amber, then the whole world seemed to be dancing color, and she knew she was on her way again. On her way and in trouble.

She fought to remember what she had to keep in her mind: the year 2061 and an unguarded timeway. Desperately she tried to fix it in her brain as the process continued and she entered the intermediate state where the world turned dark and silent and her mind seemed frozen.

She felt a great relief when the sound and the swirl of colors came back. From her previous travels, she was familiar with the blank void that always came in the middle of the trip, but somehow each time she felt the same fear that she would be lost forever in that black silence. Now she prepared herself for immediate action once she arrived. Jesse and Neil would be waiting for her and they would have to take off running down the long corridors of the timeway building if they had any hope of escape. She didn't allow herself to even think of the possibility that she might be coming into a well-guarded timeway and immediate capture.

The first thing she saw was the thick iron bars that encased the timeway. The next was her brother grinning at her. "Hurry." She saw his lips move, forming the word, but heard no sound.

As soon as she felt herself standing firmly on her own two feet, she jumped down from the timeway. It was unguarded. No one was in sight and the great gates stood open.

Jesse grabbed her hand. "Come on, let's get out of here."

They ran, staying close together even though Jeanette knew that Jesse, accustomed to the outdoors life of the frontier, could easily have outdistanced the other two. She also knew he wouldn't think of leaving them behind.

They were three-quarters of the way down the long gray corridor and light glimmered dimly at the end of it. Jeanette knew they'd come the right way and soon they'd be outside. She couldn't wait to get out of this labyrinth of a building with its twisting look-alike corridors. "We're almost there," she gasped breathlessly.

Jesse nodded, frowning as he jogged along almost effortlessly. "Something funny about this. Don't like it."

"Why not?" It was hard to talk when she could hardly get her breath. "It's what you planned. An unguarded day on the timeway."

"Didn't expect it to be this unguarded."

"Guess we were just lucky." Neil seemed to be having as much trouble running and talking at the same time as his sister.

"Never did place much confidence in luck."

Jesse shook his head, slowing slightly as they approached the exit.

Suddenly Jeanette saw movement, just the flicker of something brown at the edge of the opening into the outdoors.

Jesse saw it at the same time. "It's a trap!" he yelled. "Run back the other way!"

Abruptly sirens wailed all around them and they heard the sound of shouting and then the pounding of many feet. They were being chased.

Already tired from the long run down the corridor, Jeanette whirled about sharply, new adrenaline pumping into her system from sheer fear. She ran as hard as she could, only to look around and realize she was running alone.

Where were Jesse and Neil? Still running, she looked back. Neil was on the ground. Evidently he'd stumbled and fallen. Jesse was already headed back to help him. She stopped and turned to run toward her fallen brother.

He scrambled to his feet, but the huge brown figures of the protectors were almost on him. "No," he yelled. "Keep going. Keep running. I'll get away. They can't keep me."

They had him! Abruptly, Jesse, seeing his rescue mission doomed to failure, wheeled about and headed back in her direction. He grabbed at her arm so forcefully that she felt it was being pulled from her body and dragged her along with him.

"We've got to help Neil," she cried.

"Can't. Not now." He forced her to run.

She could hear the pounding feet of the protectors just behind them. Then Jesse was dragging her, diving with her into an opening in the wall. They were in one of the long, tubelike devices used for local transportation in the guardians' world.

She felt herself swept along, her arm in Jesse's strong grip, until they were deposited gently in another building with long gray corridors identical to the first. "They saw us go into the tube," she shouted. "They'll follow us here."

He nodded grimly. Looking around, Jeanette saw that this must be some sort of junction for the transportation units. The wall was lined with more than a dozen different tube entrances. "We'll keep traveling," he said. "They won't know which way we went from here."

Without taking time to discuss it further, they hurried to enter another tube opening, choosing at random. Jeanette closed her eyes, thinking as she always did when she traveled the tubes that it was like being a speck caught up in the vacuum hose that Lillian insisted be used so regularly back at home.

But when they landed again and he made her enter another tube, she felt her mind beginning to emerge from the stunned shock that had encased it since she first realized they were running right into a trap. Neil! What could be happening to him?

Once they again stood on solid ground, she willed herself to relax and look around. Instead of being in one of the gray halls or even in the barren urban landscape where the guardians were kept busy looking after humanity, they were on a sunny hillside, looking down on a very normal-looking small town. It had houses, stores, streets, and a profusion of flower gardens and trees. The paved roadway was only just down the hill from them and it wound away through distant hills. She could hear the faint hum of a car coming toward them.

The change was so abrupt that for a moment she couldn't think. "Jesse, where are we?"

She heard him sigh. "I reckon we're in one of those fake places where they kept people in QL47's time."

Of course. She'd almost forgotten. Last fall when the guardians had been attempting to fit them into the world of 2061, they'd been introduced to a number of such colonies, including a picturesque little fishing village and what had seemed to be a moon base settlement. But none had turned out to be real. Instead each was like an elaborate movie set—with real rooms, houses, and people behind the facade. This was the way the guardians had invented to keep their human charges happy.

The thought gave her a panicky feeling. She turned toward the tube entrance and, with no surprise, saw that it didn't look like an entrance at all. Shrubbery had closed across it so that only an apparently solid wall of greenery grew across the hill. Her mouth grew dry as she remembered something else.

"Don't see why we can't just stay here for a while," Jesse said. "We won't be so noticeable where there are other people instead of just those robots like QL47 and the others, and it'll give us a chance to get our bearings and figure out what to do next."

Instead of answering she pushed at the brush, trying to find the opening. No matter how she searched, it wouldn't appear.

Jesse watched her curiously. "What are you doing?"

Finally, she turned to him, her efforts fruitless. "Don't you remember, Jesse? QL47 told us that anyone could come in on the tubes to these communities, but only the guardians could give the coordinates to get out."

He stared at her, realization clouding his face. He dug at the bushes, but even though he was pulling them out by the roots, he didn't find the entrance either.

"We've come in a one-way door," Jeanette whispered.

"There's got to be a way out. Maybe it's like the timeway and we just have to give it mental coordinates." He closed his eyes, touched his hands to the sides of his head, and tried to send mental images.

"I don't think it's the same, Jesse. The timeway was built originally by humans and fell into the control of the guardians later. These little isolation communities were designed by the guardians. I don't think they intended for any humans to get out alone."

Jesse opened his eyes again, the look of panic gone. "We've gotten out of some difficult places before."

She smiled. "So we have." She didn't mention Neil's predicament again. Right now there was nothing they could do.

He got to his feet. "Shall we go exploring then?"

She nodded. They started down the hill together. It had been winter when they left home, but here it seemed like the perfect spring day. A warm breeze touched their faces and ruffled their hair, and she could hear the sound of birds singing somewhere in the distance. She couldn't help wondering if it was always spring here.

At the edge of the hill, they followed the road toward the little town. After a short walk, they saw a sign. It said GREEN VALLEY.

"Must be the name of this place."

Jesse nodded. "Guess so."

"Wonder which state it's in."

"I have a feeling they don't fool with ideas like states anymore. Not states or governments or anything like that. Don't forget, the guardians run things here."

She nodded. It would be difficult to forget about the guardians. She remembered what QL47 had said about them, that they were a type of robot invented to protect humanity from itself so that the powerful weapons inventive men and women had developed would not destroy the whole world. Apparently it had been a good idea at first, but was this the end? People kept in make-believe communities like toys in a dollhouse!

Jeanette turned to see a shiny pink object coming down the road. "It's a car, I think," she said doubtfully.

They moved to the edge of the road to let it pass, and as it drew opposite them, Jeanette could see that it was indeed an automobile, though unlike those she was accustomed to seeing on the streets at home.

It was the soft pink of a baby's ribbon, but its design was that of cars built earlier in the century. Mentally she made a correction: earlier in *her* century. It was built in blocky fashion and had running boards and what Jeanette had heard her grandmother describe as a rumble seat in the back. "It looks like a Model A or a Model T . . . or something like that," she told Jesse, adding apologetically, "I've never paid much attention to cars, but they made something like that way back. But the ones then weren't pink. They were black."

A pretty blond girl at the wheel of the car waved a large floppy hat at them in friendly fashion and blew a comical-sounding horn.

Jesse and Jeanette waved back.

The car came to a stop. The girl in the car turned to look back at them. "Would you like a ride?"

Jesse looked questioningly at Jeanette. She shrugged. "Normally I wouldn't hitchhike, it's too dangerous. But nothing about our being here is safe."

"Maybe we can kind of blend in with the local people and the guardians won't know we're here."

She nodded. "Thanks so much. We'd love a ride," she called.

The girl's smile was wide and friendly. "I

haven't seen you before. You must have just arrived."

Jeanette climbed in beside the girl and Jesse got in back. They took off at a speed that must have reached a high, Jeanette guessed, of at least twenty miles an hour! And this was the advanced, latter half of the twenty-first century.

"You just can't tell about progress," she muttered.

"I beg your pardon," the girl said.

"Oh, it's nothing. I talk to myself sometimes."

The girl smiled, her light blue eyes radiating a gentle kindness. "That's not uncommon among the people who come here, but after a while they settle right down."

"You have a lot of newcomers then?"

"Quite a few, though they're usually older people."

"I'm sure you're curious about how my friend and I came to be here."

"No, I'm hardly ever curious." The girl smiled. "It isn't in my nature."

Jeanette blinked. She thought everyone had a certain amount of natural curiosity. It seemed a healthy sign of intelligence. "You probably want to know our names."

"If you'd like to tell me."

Jeanette glanced back at Jesse. "I'm Jeanette Lacy and my friend is Jesse Lansden." The minute she'd spoken she wondered if she should have given their real names.

"I'm Charity Patience Clark," the girl said.

This time Jeanette stared. "Charity Patience?"

"It's a family name. My papa prefers old-fashioned things."

If she hadn't known better, Jeanette would have guessed that she and Jesse had gotten caught up in a time warp again. This place seemed more past than future tense. She had to remind herself of the guardians' purpose. There were many little places like this, each one distinctive in character, all of them imitations of some real place, highly desired by certain personalities.

They were approaching the outskirts of town. "You'll like Green Valley," Charity Patience said. "The guardians say it's a regular rest cure."

"You know about the guardians then?"

"Of course, I do, silly. Everybody knows about them. They take care of things. Things . . . you know . . . that are too complicated for people here. When my car stopped working, the guardians fixed it."

"What was wrong with your car?"

"I don't know. It just wouldn't go anymore and the guardians fixed it."

"But couldn't someone here in town repair it for you? Surely you have an auto-mechanic shop?"

"No." Charity Patience shook her head. "In fact, I don't even know what that is."

They drove down streets that might indeed have come from a movie set. It was like Hollywood's vision of a small town early in the century, Jeanette thought. But the century would have been the twentieth, not the twenty-first. Quaint little shops dotted the main street, flowers bloomed all over the place, and right in the middle of town was a picture-perfect town square from which strains of music wafted as if a band played, though she saw no music makers anywhere in sight.

It was, she decided, really creepy.

"There is one person in town who likes to fix things," Charity Patience announced suddenly.

"Really?"

She nodded. "He's only been here a few months, but he says funny things and makes lots of people mad. My papa talks about asking the guardians to make him leave. He says Van Lee has been upsetting everybody."

Van Lee. The name seemed to strike a familiar chord in Jeanette's brain.

"He's a very strange person. He makes me feel most uncomfortable because he's always saying such odd things."

Van Lee . . . Van Lee . . . Jeanette's brain was on a search-and-identify mission. Where could she have heard that name before?

"Anyway, if I know Van, he'll be teaching today. He won't let anybody else have a turn." Charity Patience's pretty lips formed a graceful pout.

"He's grown up then?"

"Gracious no, he's younger than either of us." She gave Jeanette an appraising glance. "You look to be about my age."

Jeanette started to say she was fifteen, then remembered the barely celebrated birthday. "I'm sixteen."

"That's close. I'm seventeen. Van is only eight."

Jeanette was beginning to feel like her brain was caught in a blender. "And he's your teacher?"

"I told you he insisted. Van is extremely pushy."

"But don't you have adult teachers?"

"Not anymore. Everybody got bored with it. Papa did it for a while, but he said teaching was such a regular thing and there wasn't much point in it. I must say, Van doesn't seem to get bored, but he does make all the rest of us feel distinctly odd with the things he says."

They pulled up to a stop in front of what looked like a school, though a very different kind than the modern high school Jeanette attended. It was a single-story red-brick building, surrounded by huge old shade trees. On one end was a small playground with a few swings, a slide, and a couple of seesaws. Half a dozen small children played on the equipment.

Jeanette counted eleven other vehicles parked adjacent to Charity Patience's pink automobile; all of them looked like facsimiles of early cars.

"You do want to go to school with me, don't you?" Charity Patience's blue eyes looked directly at her.

"Don't suppose we have any choice about going to school."

"Well, of course, we do. Nobody is going to make you do anything in Green Valley. This is a free country, for goodness sake, but all the young people are here. There isn't much else to do."

"I'm anxious to see this school," Jeanette told her. She hopped out of the car, her eyes widening slightly as Charity Patience also descended.

Charity was wearing a long, full-skirted dress that belonged to an era much earlier than the vintage automobile. They really did like things old-fashioned here!

Jesse came around to join her and they followed their hostess toward the front door. "Jesse," Jeanette whispered hurriedly. "Do you remember ever hearing about anyone named Van Lee?"

He stared at her for a moment. "I recall hearing the name."

"So do I, but the name is stuck in my brain and I can't remember where or when I heard it."

"It was when we first arrived in this place, when they took us before the court and we met QL47 and were placed in his custody. Don't you remember, they said this Van Lee character was young like us, but that he was some kind of terrible criminal, that he used the timeways to cause all sorts of trouble."

"That's it." Jeanette smiled triumphantly. "That's where we heard his name."

"So what is this all about?"

Charity Patience paused to allow them to enter the building ahead of her. Jeanette leaned close to Jesse to whisper, "I have a feeling we're about to meet another time traveler."

CHAPTER THREE

"Charity Patience," Jeanette asked, "aren't people going to think we're dressed strangely in these clothes?" She indicated her coverall with the flick of one hand. "I mean if people here dress the way you do . . ."

"Most newcomers are dressed as you are, but of course they soon find they prefer something more attractive. Except Van Lee; he likes to be different, I think." The disapproval that had been in Charity's voice before when she spoke of the boy was heightened.

"Van Lee is the name of the teacher," Jeanette responded to Jesse's questioning look. "He's eight years old."

They walked down the empty halls of the old-fashioned-looking school and Jeanette felt an angry impatience to be out of this place, rescuing her brother and finding QL47. This was only supposed to be the first stop on the journey to help Amy and the aliens being slaughtered in another time. Right now they seemed to be making no progress.

It was not a large school, but even so there didn't seem to be anybody in the classrooms. "Where are the students?" she asked.

"These rooms are for the younger children," Charity Patience explained. "And they prefer to have outdoor play most of the day."

"Recess all the time! Neil would've liked that." Jeanette couldn't help thinking this was a most unusual school.

As they approached the end of the hall, the sound of shouting voices reached them. "Van is at it again," Charity Patience said. "He's always causing a disturbance."

No one glanced their way as they entered the classroom and Jeanette got a chance to look the situation over without being observed. She counted eleven students seated at their desks, four girls and seven boys. The girls were all dressed in some variation of the costume that Charity Patience wore and the boys had on old-fashioned suits with string ties and shiny black shoes. Only the boy at the front of the room was different. But then, she was prepared for Van Lee to be somewhat unlike the others.

Like Neil, he'd chosen red for his coverall. Neither boy, apparently, wished to remain in the background, Jeanette thought with a private grin. He was small even for eight, a little on the skinny side, and his curly dark hair was cut close to his head; his strangely light eyes seemed almost amber. Even though he was talking when they entered, Jeanette was sure that he noticed their entrance.

"The real trouble is that you're all asleep in this backwater place," he said. "You're a bunch of rip-off artists who've given up on life. You've let the machines take over."

Charity Patience was standing right next to her and Jeanette could feel her quiver with sudden anger. "That is a lie. You've said before that our wonderful guardians were mechanical. It simply isn't true."

The boy's attention focused on the three of them. He didn't say anything; he simply studied them through narrowed eyes.

What a brat! Jeanette couldn't remember when she'd taken as instant a dislike to anyone as to this Van Lee. He was years younger than the teenagers he was lecturing and yet he talked to them as though they were stupid. He might be intelligent, but that didn't make him better than everyone else.

He raised dark eyebrows in something of a sneer. "Newcomers?"

The other students turned around. It was to them that Charity Patience spoke, her voice trembling with barely controlled anger. "Meet Jesse and Jeanette," she said. "They just arrived."

They were warmly welcomed by the others and Jeanette felt herself siding with them already. Funny that it seemed like they'd walked into a battle scene!

"Time to get back to business," Van Lee announced, scowling at those who'd just entered as though they were intruders.

Jeanette heard mutterings from the group, but nobody challenged the bossy little boy's authority.

"We were talking about being in charge," he went on. "Before I'm much older, I plan to be in charge of Green Valley."

"But we don't need you," Charity Patience objected. "We have the guardians."

"But I want to be in charge. I like running things."

Obviously it was very hard for Charity Patience to argue publicly this way. She looked to Jeanette as though seeking support. Jeanette smiled at her and she seemed to gain the courage she needed. "We don't want you to be in charge."

The boy folded his thin arms across his chest. "But you won't stop me. You won't do anything. People in Green Valley don't ever do anything."

"We'll get the guardians to stop you," Charity Patience insisted. "They'll take care of you."

"I'm too smart for that bunch of metal monsters," the boy boasted.

Jeanette's first impression, that here was someone she could intensely dislike, was confirmed. Van Lee was a spoiled rotten egotistical brat!

Jesse got to his feet, his lanky height making a strong contrast to the small boy at the front of the room. Jesse leaned back slightly, resting his weight against the edge of a desk in a very nonthreatening manner. "Seems to me that the best way for people to decide who looks after the town's business is by everybody getting together and voting. Neighbors usually have a fair idea of who's best able to take on that kind of responsibility."

He sat down again. Van Lee looked at him as though he'd just been given new food for thought. "That's fine," he said, "as long as everybody votes for me."

"But what if they don't want to vote for you," Jeanette objected.

"I'll make them!"

Jeanette leaned close to Jesse to whisper in his ear. "Sounds like he'd make a great dictator."

"No whispering allowed!" the boy shouted. He pointed an accusing finger at Jeanette. "You will repeat what you just said aloud so everyone can hear."

Jesse shook his head. "No, I don't believe she will do that." His lazy drawl was as soft and easy as ever, but his mouth was set in a firm line.

Van glared at him. "I'll have to make her then."

This time Jeanette folded her arms. "Just try."

He looked at them both as though he'd like to throw them from the classroom. But then he shook his head. "You're lucky I don't want to make you talk. Elsewise, I'd force you to do it."

Jesse laughed softly and the boy's face reddened. "Everybody go home," the boy announced suddenly. "School's over for today."

Again a soft murmur of protest rippled across the group. "But we were going to have a school dance," a boy protested, "with refreshments."

"Dance is canceled. Go home."

To Jeanette's surprise, the students obeyed. Even Charity Patience, who must be some sort of rebel by the standards of this place, got up and followed the others out. At the doorway, she turned to smile weakly at Jesse and Jeanette. "If you like, you can stay at my house until the guardians tell you where you'll live. We're at the corner of Sunshine and Sweetbriar streets. It's the lavender house."

Jeanette thanked her with sincerity. She'd thought Charity Patience a bit of a dim bulb at first meeting, but she'd been the only one who'd even attempted to stand up to the junior-grade tyrant at the front of the school.

"We'll be along in a little," Jesse said. "We want to talk to Mr. Lee here first."

Charity Patience nodded and left.

"I don't want to talk to you," Van Lee told Jesse.

"Then you can listen. First thing we want to say is we know about you."

"What's to know?"

"That you don't belong here at all. That you're a time traveler."

Another memory suddenly popped into Jeanette's mind. "You're Van Lee from nineteen ninety-two and you've caused all sorts of trouble."

Van looked a little proud of himself. "I was born in nineteen ninety-two and I was only six when I started time walking and I guess you could say I've stirred things up a little."

"You needn't sound so pleased with yourself about it."

"Why not? These people just sit around and

expect the guardians to look after them. They don't have any ambition, they don't even wonder about anything. I'll bet they don't even dream when they sleep at night. They're just like cattle in a pen, expecting to be cared for."

It was, Jeanette thought, an interesting analysis. Van Lee might be a little monster, but obviously he was also extremely bright. This was not exactly an average eight-year-old.

"So you think people have stopped dreaming?"

He nodded, really meeting her eyes for the first time. "Yes, and it seems to me when people quit dreaming, sleeping and awake, when they can't even imagine wonderful and terrible things happening, then they're not going to make anything happen. They're not really people anymore. They're just sort of like pets."

"I had a really nice kitten when I was a little girl." Jeanette couldn't help protesting the slur on pets.

Van sat down on the edge of the teacher's desk. "I'm sure you'd think those kids that were just in here were nice too. But they're not quite real people, not anymore."

Jeanette was conscious of Jesse, sitting quietly at her side, leaving the debate to her. What did he think of all this? "So you're trying to turn them into people again?"

Van shrugged. "Not me. Why bother when this is such a golden opportunity. I'll be running Green Valley and several other communities just like it by the time I'm twenty. And when I'm thirty, well, look out!"

Jeanette could almost believe it and the thought

made her shiver. This little boy seemed to have set himself on the path to becoming a magnificently terrible person. Obviously he had the potential to fulfill his dream.

Now he looked at them with that narrowing of his eyes that she was beginning to learn was characteristic. "You don't belong here. You're not like the others."

"You know we just arrived."

"No, I mean you're not products of the guardian society. You know how to think."

Jeanette laughed a little uneasily. She wasn't at all sure she wanted to trust any important secrets in his hands. "Surely there are a few exceptions, a few rebellious souls who just can't be made to fit in."

"Oh, sure. They get reconditioned. And if that doesn't work, then they're sent to the prison camp."

Jeanette looked around a little nervously. "I thought this place was a prison. There's no way out."

"You can get out. It's not easy, but there are ways if you're smart enough. But the prison camp is different. The guardians get really serious because they think the people locked up there are going to hurt everybody else. They were designed to protect people."

"We know." Jeanette looked meaningfully at Jesse. This boy had just said he knew how to escape Green Valley. But she knew better than to approach the problem directly. Most likely if they asked him for help, he'd have great fun denying it. He was obviously not a boy who delighted in being helpful. "We've run up against the guardians a few times ourselves."

"We did meet one who tried to help us, though." Jesse spoke for the first time in several minutes. "So that proves that even the guardians aren't all bad."

Van Lee laughed mirthlessly. "This guy really took you in, didn't he?"

"QL47 honestly befriended us," Jeanette protested. "He helped us escape and get back home."

"Then what are you doing here?"

"We're trying to find him and my brother. They're both in trouble and need help."

"Not here?"

"No." Jeanette gestured vaguely toward the hills. "Out there in the guardians' world."

"You don't want to go back out there. It's a really tough place."

"So we discovered. They were chasing us."

"Oh, I've been chased a few times. The thing you've got in your favor is this programming they've got against hurting people. They'd rather see one of their own destroyed than have you as much as stub your toe."

"And you've learned to use that?" Jeanette asked.

"I'm not stupid and I've been bouncing around here for over two years. At first I was running all over the timeways, popping in here and there. But then I saw the biggest advantage was right here. It's my best chance to run things."

"And that's what you want to do?"

"Sure, it's what anybody with brains would

want. I mean if you're the big boss, you can have anything."

"Where are you from and how did you discover the timeway in the first place?"

He didn't answer, but studied her with narrowed eyes. "You're time travelers too, aren't you?"

Jeanette didn't answer. After a moment, Jesse nodded.

"I thought you didn't belong here. Well, go back where you belong before you mess things up for me."

"Nothing we'd like better," Jesse assured him, "but first we've got to find Jeanette's brother and talk to QL47. There's something we've got to ask him."

"About what?"

"Afraid that's private."

Van looked as though he wanted to protest, but after a moment of studying Jesse, who didn't appear to be about to back down, he changed tactics. "Maybe I could help you find your friends."

"Why would you do that?" Jeanette was suspicious. She was sure this kid hadn't done anything just to be helpful in his entire life.

"Because you're going to wreck things for me if you stay. You'll bumble around and do stupid things and get the guardians to pay particular attention to Green Valley."

"I should think the things you were saying to those kids awhile back would have made them upset."

He shrugged. "Just talk. The guardians don't

care what we say, not as long as everybody's happy and nobody rocks the boat. And in the meantime, I'm beginning to build my power base."

"Maybe you didn't notice, Van, but those kids didn't like you."

"Doesn't matter. They're beginning to be afraid of me. That's what counts. When I take over, nobody will dare oppose me."

He was, Jeanette decided, a very frightening little boy. He could also prove quite useful in their present situation. "But you're willing to help us get out of Green Valley?"

"I told you I would. I don't want you messing things up for me, but we'll have to wait until tonight when it gets dark. In the meantime, go on over to the Clarks' house and try to fit in. In other words, act stupid."

"That's unkind, Van. Charity Patience isn't exactly stupid."

"No, what's worse is that she was born smart. She's put her brain on hold ever since, like everybody else in this place." He nodded toward the door. "Now, if you want my help, you'll do as I say and keep a low profile."

Jeanette took a step toward the door, but Jesse didn't move. "I'm not sure we want your help. I'm not at all sure you can be trusted."

"See!" Van allowed himself a slow, cynical smile. "You're not stupid. But the reason you can trust me is because we both want the same thing. You want out and I'm real anxious to get you out."

Jesse nodded. "Guess we don't have much choice. Where will we meet?"

"I'll come by the Clark house for you after it gets dark."

Jeanette and Jesse left the school together and started walking back toward the center of town. "Not very many children in the school," she said. "Not even for a town this size."

"Maybe most of them stayed home." He seemed preoccupied.

"Maybe. You don't like having to rely on Van Lee for help, do you? I can't blame you. He's a really rotten little kid."

"A sad little kid, if you ask me. How did anybody get to looking at the world like that in only eight years?"

"I hadn't thought of that. He does have a miserable viewpoint on things. All he sees is how he can work people and situations to his own advantage. A real potential Hitler type."

He looked interested. "Who?"

She shook her head. "Somebody after your time. Not anyone you'd want to know about."

"I feel sorry for him. Wish there was some way to help. I'll bet he's never had a friend."

"If he did, he'd just take advantage in some way. Come on, Jesse, the kid's hopeless."

"Nobody's that, Jeanette." He smiled at her.

They walked slowly in the sun-warmed afternoon, hearing the soft sound of music from the town square. "This isn't such a bad place, if it didn't feel so phony."

"That's because we know what it really is and that the guardians are back of it."

"Here's Sunshine Street." She pointed to a sign. "Real positive names they have for the streets here. I suppose the guardians thought them up and they didn't want anything downbeat."

"You're beginning to sound like Van."

"Well, in a way he's right, Jesse. I doubt these people are creative enough to name their own streets."

The lavender house was just ahead. It was a neat two-story with lacy white trim. Jesse walked ahead of Jeanette to knock on the door.

A middle-aged man dressed in an old-fashioned business suit answered. "Good afternoon," he said. "You must be Charity Patience's new friends. Come in. Come in."

His tone was friendly and the welcome was warm. He was, he explained, Charity Patience's papa. A moment later, her mama, a little dumpling of a woman in a long dress covered with a frilly apron, came in to greet them as well.

"My, but it's nice to have company." She beamed at them. "Especially young company. What would you like for dinner?"

Jeanette was a little embarrassed at this request for menu suggestions. "Whatever you've planned will be fine."

"No, dear, we want you to have whatever you like. In fact, you might even want to enter the order yourself."

Of course! Jeanette had forgotten that even food preparation was in the hands of the guardians, just another of those little details of life with which humanity no longer had to bother.

Requests for food, clothing, or anything else only had to be made electronically and the desired items were delivered through a special dispenser.

"Perhaps our visitors would prefer to have some nice cold lemonade first and then we can talk over what we'd like for dinner," her husband suggested. He left the room, returning only a couple of minutes later with a tray that contained tall, frosted glasses. Charity Patience came just behind him, carrying a plate of cookies.

Refreshments were handed around and everyone found seats in the comfortable parlor of the Clark home. Feeling a little awkward, Jeanette tried to make conversation. "I'd gotten the impression from your daughter that newcomers aren't unusual in Green Valley, Mr. Clark, but you say visitors are uncommon?"

"No, no, my dear. Lots of visitors. Green Valley's such a pleasant place, you see. People come here to unwind and relax. It's young visitors such as yourselves that are rare."

"We have so few children in Green Valley," Mrs. Clark said, sounding sad. "And I always did like children."

"But they're such a lot of trouble." Her husband's voice was comforting. "Always needing attention and creating untidyness wherever they go. Not that Charity Patience was like that."

"Oh no," her mother agreed, "our daughter was quite exceptional."

Charity Patience looked, Jeanette thought, a little embarrassed. She tried to change the subject to spare the other girl's feelings. "We noticed you didn't have many students at the school.

You must have a very low population of school-aged children."

"Not many children," Mrs. Clark agreed sadly.

"But then, life is much neater without children," Mr. Clark added. "And each generation, we have fewer children. The town is growing smaller as the old-timers die out."

Mrs. Clark sighed gently. "It makes me feel badly just to think about it."

"Now dear, it is our duty in life to be happy. We have everything we want. We're so well taken care of here in Green Valley. It would be a crime to complain."

"You're quite right," Mrs. Clark agreed with her husband. "I'm happy. I'm extremely happy."

But Jeanette couldn't help thinking that nobody she'd met so far in Green Valley seemed anything but vaguely depressed. "Do you dream?" she asked Charity Patience with unplanned abruptness.

"Do I what?" The golden-haired beauty seemed startled.

"When you go to sleep at night, do you dream? Or in the daytime, do you daydream?"

"Well, of course, sometimes, everyone dreams. But if I really have trouble sleeping, I take medicine. The guardians give it to us. They don't want us to be bothered by nightmares."

"But dreams aren't . . ." Jeanette broke off in midsentence. What was the point of this? She was beginning to sound like Van, trying to argue away a whole society. Right now, she'd better concentrate on her own problems.

* * *

They ate dinner with the Clarks, and as the evening darkened, they went out on the front porch where Mr. Clark brought out a freezer of "homemade" vanilla ice cream, supplied by the dispenser.

It was nicely old-fashioned and Jeanette couldn't help wondering if Jesse didn't feel more at home here than he had in a long time. She went over to where he was leaning against the porch railing, staring out into the night. "Fireflies," he said.

She watched the tiny lights winking off and on out in the darkness and sniffed the moist, warm air of spring. "A person could really settle in here," she said.

"And be happy, happy." His tone was sarcastic.

"Then you're ready to go?"

He nodded.

She tucked her fingers around his arm, hoping they looked like a courting couple, and they strolled out into the night together. They were only a few feet away from the glow cast from the porch light when they heard Van's whisper.

"Come on, let's get going. We've got to hurry because the guardians are already on to you. They know you're here."

CHAPTER FOUR

They followed him away from the house, carefully avoiding the light cast from neighboring homes and walking in the dark on the other side of the street. "How can they know we're here?"

"Hush! We'll talk when we get out of town."

Jeanette stayed close to Jesse's side as they followed Van. He led them quickly through town and down the dark, unlighted road that led away from it.

"Are we going back to the entrance?" Jeanette asked. "Because, if we are, you might as well know that we already tried to get through and couldn't."

"You sure do talk a lot."

Jesse stopped abruptly. "No need to be rude."

Van glared at him. "You want my help, don't you?"

"Not if you're going to talk to Jeanette like

that. We'll go back to town and work things out our own way."

"And have you mess up more than you already have? Don't you think you put somebody wise when you let the Clarks order two extra meals? The guardians aren't stupid, you know."

Jeanette decided *stupid* was his favorite word. "You've been living here. Surely you eat."

"Yeah, but I've got a fake identity. As far as the guardians are concerned, I belong."

"It didn't occur to us that they'd notice an extra meal or two. Surely they don't keep such close count on everything."

"You bet they do. A little difference in food intake and they're down here checking to see if one of their precious charges is sick or something."

"And you think the extra meals have made them suspicious?"

"Sure, they're looking for you. I was over at the mayor's house when the inquiry came in."

"The mayor?"

"Sure, people take turns if they want to. Most of 'em think it's too much trouble. Anyway, the guardians are asking questions about strangers in town. They'll have some protectors down here checking before you can turn around twice."

"Then we'd better get out of here."

Van didn't answer as he started on down the road. But after they'd walked about a quarter of a mile, he left the road behind and headed south.

"The entrance was in the other direction," Jesse said.

"That's not where we're going. You'd have to

be one of the guardians to get that thing to work."

Jeanette couldn't help thinking wearily that it would be nice if Van tried to be a little friendly. His tone was always so scornful, as though he thought everyone beneath his contempt. She followed, finding it increasingly hard to keep walking. "I'm tired."

She felt Jesse's hand rest briefly against her back. "It's been a long time since we've had any rest."

She tried to calculate. They'd left home at nightfall, but it had been bright day when they'd arrived here. Somewhere they'd lost a night's sleep. She was beginning to feel it.

They talked quietly as they followed Van across the hills, wondering what Neil was doing and if he was frightened. "I'm sure he knows we're doing our best to help him."

Jeanette nodded. "I keep being afraid they'll do something awful to him."

"The guardians wouldn't hurt a human except by accident, or to keep him from hurting another human. The worst punishment they can imagine is the web, and they only do that when they've tried everything else." Van's voice held a note of self-importance, as though he enjoyed playing the expert.

"The web? What's that?"

"Don't know exactly, but it puts you out of commission for good."

"How come you know so much about the guardians, Van?"

"I'm smart. I keep my eyes open, and like I

told you, I've been in and out of their custody since I was six."

"You place a lot of importance on intelligence, don't you?" Jesse asked thoughtfully.

"Sure, it *is* important. It's what gives you a head start on everybody else. I know I'm smart and I mean to make the most of it."

"Well, we appreciate your helping us," Jesse said quietly, "no matter what the motivation."

"I told you I'm just doing myself a favor." The boy sounded almost angry.

"He doesn't want to be friendly," Jeanette whispered to Jesse.

"I'm not so sure of that. Maybe he just doesn't know how."

She smiled at him. "You're a perpetual optimist, Jesse Lansden."

"You two have to keep one fact in mind," Van called to them. "Once we get to the line, you're on your own. I'm going back to Green Valley and you can take your own risks."

"The line? Is that where we get out of the community?"

"Yep. There's an electrical barrier, but I know how to short that out. It's not too hard. They don't have to worry about the average citizen trying to escape. They're all too happy living back there in Green Valley." His tone was ironic. "But just remember, they have a terrific monitoring system and they'll spot the break in the line right away. You've got to clear out fast. And if you're caught, just don't mention my name to anybody."

Jeanette found herself growing increasingly tired

as they trudged on. By the time they reached what Van called the line, she was almost too exhausted to think. The barrier looked like an elaborate metal fence, intricately woven so that it reached from the ground to a height that was several feet over her head. Its design was such that she was sure she could slip her feet in between the strands and scale it. She started toward it.

"Wait!" Van whispered loudly. "If you touch that thing, you'll get the shock of your life."

She stared helplessly at it. "Then what are we to do?"

"Wait here. Every half mile or so, there's a controlling unit. I'll walk until I find one of those. I'm sure I can adjust it so this section of the fence will go out. I've done it before so I could go in and out of Green Valley without anybody guessing. The guardians just think it malfunctions."

He started off, disappearing into the darkness. "The protectors check these barriers regularly," he called, still speaking in a loud whisper. "So if you see anybody coming, hide!"

Jesse and Jeanette stood together, waiting until the sound of the boy's footsteps died away. "Do you think he'll give us away?"

"Jeanette, I'd say it would be real hard to predict what Van Lee would do. What I'd suggest is that we find a hiding place right now so we can keep an eye on him when he comes back and make sure he's alone."

"But he hates the guardians. He wouldn't give us away to them."

"He might if he thought it was to his advantage."

He was right, of course. Jeanette started looking around for the best shelter, but Jesse spotted it before she did. They crept cautiously over to a thick cluster of bushes that clung to the side of the hill.

"This'll do fine. Just let me crawl in first to make sure it's safe."

Jeanette didn't even bother to argue. He was never going to get over the idea that he was supposed to protect her, even though she'd certainly come to his aid as many times as he'd helped her. His trouble was that he had been born in the wrong century.

"It's safe," he called in a muffled voice.

Jeanette got down on her hands and knees and crawled through the narrow opening in the prickly bushes. Inside she found a large enough space for them both to huddle. She yawned. "I'm so tired that I don't know if I'll be able to stay awake until Van gets back."

"No reason we can't get a little sleep. Nobody would guess we're hiding in here and Van will know to call. When we hear his voice, we'll peek out and make sure it's not a trap."

"If you're sure." Jeanette curled up in a little ball, resting her head on one arm while Jesse tried to stretch out in the limited space, his long legs sticking into the bushes. "I'm so exhausted I could sleep on a rock if I had to."

But he was already, instantly asleep. She couldn't help wondering if it was really wise for them to catch a nap like this in the middle of dangerous territory. She was determined to stay awake, listening for the approach of danger. She would just close her eyes and rest a little. . . .

Tired as she was, she didn't fall into heavy sleep, but floated in troubling, turbulent dreams. In her dreams she was reunited with Amy, facing the battle of 2099 when the aliens landed, only to find themselves attacked by the guardians, who saw them as a threat to their human charges. In the dream she tried to run away with Amy as rays of light pierced the bubblelike ships of Amy's people. Screams of the injured sounded around them. "Run, Jeanette," Amy shouted. "You must hurry or we'll all die!"

Jeanette awakened abruptly to find her body wet with perspiration. She rolled over. Jesse was still asleep.

Carefully, so as not to awaken him, she started crawling out of the bushes. How long had she been asleep? Had they been so deeply unconscious that Van had come back, called for them, and then, thinking they'd left, gone on?

She was nearly to the edge of the bushes when she heard voices. "I left them right here."

She recognized Van's voice and her heart started racing. So Jesse's guess had been right. Van had decided to betray them. She lay very still, hoping Jesse wouldn't stir in his sleep and give them away by making some inadvertent sound.

"They've got to be here. They were both nearly too tired to move, I'm sure they haven't gone far. Besides, I told them I'd be back soon."

"They are well and unharmed?" she heard a familiar voice ask.

It was QL47! She had almost called out when a chilling thought struck her. The guardians were machines. Perhaps QL47 was only a typical tutor model. Maybe a thousand robots existed who sounded exactly like their friend. She edged closer in an attempt to see.

It was nearly morning. A faint rosy light was showing on the edge of the horizon and by that light she could see two silhouetted figures, one of them short and the other tall.

"It was quite a coincidence my running into you that way," Van said, sounding as though he didn't believe in coincidences. "Jeanette and Jesse said you were their friend, but I didn't believe them. Besides how did you know they were here?"

"All guardians are aware of their presence in Green Valley. They would already have been recaptured, but that a plan had to be drawn so that could be accomplished without upsetting the residents. They've already been disturbed enough."

"What do you mean?" The boy's tone was almost too innocent.

"You need not think we were unaware of your presence in Green Valley either, Van Lee. You are not quite as clever as you believe."

"You're just saying that because you don't want me to believe that I really fooled you. If you'd known I was there, you would have come in after me."

"You have proved most elusive, Van Lee. Your

mental capacities are formidable. But we hoped by allowing you to spend time with the gentle people of Green Valley, some of their qualities of contentment might be absorbed into your disturbed mind. Unfortunately, we are discovering that instead the opposite is happening. They are beginning to pick up the disturbance."

"I don't think so. They're a bunch of real wood heads."

"Several of them are becoming quite disturbed. One Charity Patience Clark, for example, is almost rebellious. That's why your presence in Green Valley will no longer be tolerated by the protectors. Your removal is, of course, for your best good and for that of everyone else."

Jeanette grinned at the familiar phrase. It was one QL47 had used again and again as justification for their imprisonment last fall, but finally she'd managed to turn it against him and convince him that what was best for them and the others was to be allowed to regain their freedom.

But was this truly QL47 or simply some identical twin?

"You've got to remember our deal: I turn Jeanette and Jesse over to you, and you let me go."

"You can't go back to Green Valley."

"You don't have to tell me that. I'm not a wood head. I'll find another good spot."

"As you say. But in the meantime, you haven't turned Jeanette and Jesse over to me They don't seem to be in the vicinity."

"They're probably just hiding. What do you suppose they thought when they saw me walking up with one of the guardians? They couldn't know you were their friend."

"Very true."

Jeanette saw the tall guardian, who was dressed in the white suit that indicated his rank as tutor, look around as though surveying the territory. "There are several probable hiding places." He started walking around, coming to a stop right in front of where Jeanette lay in the bushes. She found herself staring at the back of his shoes, then almost screamed when she felt a touch on her own ankle. Jesse! He was awake.

"Jesse, Jeanette," the guardian called. "It's your old friend, QL47."

Anybody could say that. Jeanette didn't move.

"We went through a lot together. I tried to help you even though I wasn't able to complete the coordinates to get Jesse all the way home."

That was true. The guardians might have dug that information out of QL47, but it wasn't likely. Jeanette stirred restlessly, but Jesse grasped her ankle in a warning grip. Not yet, that touch seemed to communicate.

"I've come to help you. It's my fault you're here because I sent you the message asking you to help the aliens."

Neither of them moved.

"You've got to trust me. Remember that I discovered one of you is to be keeper. Would the guardians be trying to recapture you if they knew that? The coming of the time keeper is, after all, instrumental to their own development."

Jeanette allowed her face to sag weakly against the ground. Logical as always, that was QL47!

He was right. If the guardians knew who they were, everything would be different.

She felt Jesse release the strangling grip he had on her ankle. "Hi, QL47," she called, starting to climb out from the cover of the bushes.

He turned to face them, waiting unemotionally until they were both standing before him. Then he allowed himself a faint smile. "It's very good to see you again."

It was, Jeanette knew, equivalent to a joyous reunion from anyone else. QL47 wasn't one to let his feelings run away with him.

She knew that she must be grinning from ear to ear. "You can't guess how glad we are to see you, QL47. We were so afraid they'd done something terrible to you for helping us."

"They wouldn't do that. My superiors recognized that I was only responding to my programming. Once I became convinced that assisting you was the only way to act in the best interests of humanity, I had no other choice."

"And it wasn't because you learned to like us, not in the least little bit?" Jeanette teased.

"Guardians have only the emotions originally programmed into them," he assured her without a trace of humor. "We feel a general affection for all humanity, but to feel more strongly for particular individuals would not be possible."

"Oh, sure." This time Jesse was the one teasing. "But I think you kind of favor Jeanette. You treat her like she was your own daughter."

"Jeanette is unusual. I admire the faculties of her intelligence."

"Hey!" This seemed to strike a chord for Van.

"If you like brains, mine are probably three times better than hers."

QL47 regarded the younger boy with obvious disapproval. "That remains to be proven."

"Well, QL47, what happens next?" Jeanette asked. "How do we go about helping the aliens?"

"That's hard to say."

"You mean you don't know!"

He shook his head. "I only know that without intervention, they will all die, even down to the last of the infants."

Jeanette closed her eyes, thinking of Amy. She was scared for all of them, but Amy was someone she knew and cared about. "We have to do something."

"We thought sure you'd know what we needed to do, QL47," Jesse added quietly. "Seems to me we could do more damage than good by racing ahead to try to help."

"That is possible." QL47 nodded again. "That is, of course, the great risk of time intervention."

So they'd wasted their time coming here. They might as well have headed straight into the future to the day Amy's people landed. Jeanette couldn't help feeling extremely dejected. "I guess the thing to do then is try to find Neil so we can help him escape. Then we can head back to the timeway."

"Count me out," Van informed her. "I'm not going on any rescue missions."

"I can assure you no one expected you to," she told him, her tone sharpened by annoyance and fatigue. They hadn't gotten enough rest to even be thinking clearly and now they had to find a way to locate Neil.

"You will help us find my brother, won't you, QL47?"

"Of course." He started walking toward the fence and they followed him. He held the strands of fence wire, paying no attention at all to the way the wires hissed and crackled as he unwound the mesh and created a good-sized opening. "Come," he said.

Very cautiously, so as not to touch a single wire, they moved through the opening.

Once on the other side, Jeanette looked around carefully. The dim light of the dawn made surrounding objects more visible, but even so she couldn't see much. What she could see of the terrain looked much as it did on the other side, with trees and rolling hills. "Where are we now?" she asked. "Back in the guardian city?"

Van gave her the answer. "Nope, this is another place. It's a desert-type environment with the occasional oasis, a phony-looking palm tree and the whole bit. It's one of the territories I've been considering."

QL47 glanced disapprovingly at the boy. "This was meant to be a creative colony for artists and writers. I must say it hasn't been very successful."

"That's because none of these people have a creative bone left in their body. Who would with the guardians leaning over their shoulders all the time saying, 'You wouldn't want to paint something like that. It might depress someone.' I'll just bet that anyone who shows a sign of real creativity gets recultured like a shot and comes back 'normal.' "

"Sometimes reculturing doesn't work," QL47 told him coldly.

Van grinned. "I know, I've been recultured six times. I'll bet the guardians have about decided I'm a hopeless case."

"So I've heard."

To Jeanette this only seemed like another pointless detour. "But QL47, don't we need to head back to the city? That must be where they're holding Neil."

He nodded. "We will enter the tube for this colony. It's only a few yards ahead."

He led the way up the hill. They reached the crest and on the other side saw a totally different view. It was, as Van said, a desert. Sand covered the landscape, sweeping to the edge of the horizon. The rising sun sent a glimmer of varied and subtle colors dancing and glittering across the dunes.

QL47 didn't pause to admire the landscape. He led them to an outcropping of red rock that created a slight rise. Jeanette wasn't surprised when he shoved a rock aside to reveal an opening. She watched him push buttons on a small object he withdrew from his pocket.

"Guess I'll be going now," Van said, edging away from them a little hesitantly as though fearful of being stopped.

QL47 didn't look up. "You'd be well advised to be careful, Mr. Lee. The guardians feel that you've quite used up all your chances. I don't think another attempt at reculturing will be made if you fall into official hands again."

Van's face drained of color. It was the first time Jeanette had ever seen him look scared. "See you later." He half stumbled in his eagerness to get away, racing across the sand dunes.

"Thanks, Van," Jesse called.

"Oh, yeah, thanks," Jeanette added, not sure that he deserved their gratitude. He had helped them, but only because he thought it would be of personal benefit.

She looked at QL47. "Why was he so frightened by what you said?"

"He's fearful of being put out of action on a permanent basis."

"You mean killed?"

QL47's distinguished features seemed frozen with shock. "Certainly not. You know we'd never do such a thing. Death would not be in his best interest."

"But then what?"

"We'd simply arrange it so that he couldn't cause any more trouble. I feel sure that's inevitably going to happen. He's bound to be taken into custody within a day or two."

"Why didn't you turn him in?"

"Because I said I wouldn't if he helped me find you. It would not be proper to break the agreement . . . even if it might have been in Van's best interest." He looked somewhat wistfully in the direction the boy was walking. "But now, we have other concerns." He indicated the transporter tube.

"I can't wait to find Neil and make sure he's

all right." Jeanette entered the tube first, her excitement rising. She couldn't help feeling a little more optimistic about everything now that they had QL47 with them again. He was an expert about this place and time and was bound to be tremendously helpful.

The transporter tube deposited her gently at the other end and she stepped out, only to be seized from either side. She screamed as she saw that her captors wore brown uniforms. The protectors!

"Don't come, Jesse," she yelled. "Stay back. It's another trap."

But it was useless. He couldn't hear her. And seconds later when he stepped out of the tube, they grabbed for him too. She watched helplessly while he struggled, fighting with all the rough techniques that frontier life had taught him. He caught one large-sized protector right in the middle of the nose. The protector staggered for an instant, then grabbed for Jesse's arm. Another caught the boy from behind, wrapping long arms around his chest and pinning his arms to his side. Jesse continued to thrash about, trying to get loose, but it was hopeless.

"Just you wait," Jeanette threatened pointlessly. She wanted to tell them that QL47 would be here any second now and he'd take care of them. But what could he do against the two dozen or so protectors now crowding around them? She only wished she had some way of warning him so he could evade capture and the inevitable punishment he would be given for once again coming to their aid. But she was helpless.

When QL47 stepped from the transportation tube, he didn't even look surprised. He glanced around quickly, trying to locate the two of them. "You're all right?" he asked Jeanette.

When she nodded, he turned to where three protectors were trying to keep Jesse still. "Jesse?"

"I'm fine. Just help me get loose so I can show these guys how fine I am!"

"Please don't continue to struggle. No one wants to hurt you."

Slowly the horror began to grow inside Jeanette's mind. It took quite awhile for it to make sense.

Nobody had grabbed QL47, nor had he seemed surprised by the presence of the protectors.

"Do something, QL47," Jesse demanded furiously.

For once, Jeanette thought, Jesse was a little behind her in figuring things out. "Jesse, he isn't going to help us because he set this whole thing up."

Jesse's face went almost as pale as Van's had only a few minutes before. He didn't say anything; he just stared at QL47 as though trying to read his mind. The robot met his gaze with a steady look from his gray eyes.

Jesse turned his face away as though he couldn't bear to look at QL47 any longer.

"Jesse, Jeanette, it is in your best interest. I only cooperated because they made me see that I should."

Jeanette couldn't help asking some questions.

"Did they help to make you see that by reculturing you, QL47?"

"Reculturing is for humans. Guardians must have their programming corrected when problems occur."

"And they reprogrammed you?"

"Of course, they said my thinking had been confused."

The protectors stood in place like statues, allowing them to talk. Jeanette couldn't help wondering what they were waiting for. "And they knew when you sent us the message on the timeway?"

"They knew, but I wouldn't have sent anything that was untrue. They told me to send a message, but I chose what to say. Without you, the aliens will all die."

His tone was strange, drifting and uncertain. "You don't sound like yourself, QL47."

"No . . . no . . . that's why. I've become faulty, you see, defective. That's why they're sending me with you, even though it's most unusual."

"Sending us where?" Jesse shouted the question.

"A safe place where we can't hurt ourselves or others. We can't get away. No one's ever gotten away from there."

Only one place fitted that description. "The prison camp?"

"That's it. That's where we're going. We'll be very happy there, I'm sure." He looked around as though expecting someone to arrive. "You do understand, don't you, that it was only because I wanted what was best for you."

Jesse made a derisive sound, but Jeanette couldn't help responding. "We understand, QL-47," she said softly.

The individual the protectors had been waiting for strode into the scene, the protectors moving away from his path so that he could come right up to view the prisoners.

Somehow Jeanette had been certain who it would be. The large man in the brown uniform might be a machine, perhaps there were ten thousand copies just like him, but she doubted that anything could glare in quite such an evil way. Protectors, like all guardians, might be programmed with only good feelings toward human beings, but somehow this one seemed to particularly dislike them. It was, of course, their old friend, the captain of the protectors corps.

"Ha!" he said. "We finally have them. I was sure from the first time I caught them using the timeways that we had to do something serious to stop them. Now you can see, QL47, that I was right."

"I want them safe," QL47 said, frowning. "You must remember what I told you about one of them being time keeper."

"Certainly, we remember. That's why we're going to have the keeper locked up."

"But how can anybody make scientific discoveries when they're locked up?" Jeanette demanded. "Jesse can't work in a vacuum."

"Who me?" Jesse looked shocked. "I think you've got me mixed up with someone else."

"It's time to go now," the captain said. He motioned to QL47 to lead the way. Jeanette and

Jesse were lifted up by the arms and carried after him.

Suddenly QL47 came to a stop and turned to look back at them. "Don't worry about Neil," he said. "He'll be there too. We're all going to be together again."

CHAPTER FIVE

Jeanette woke up slowly, feeling vaguely that she'd just had the best sleep she'd had in ages. It was almost as though she'd been very sick and the fever had finally broken and she'd drifted into sleep where she'd had wild and delightful dreams. "Keli," she said, "you can't imagine what I dreamed."

She sat up and realized that her stepsister could not possibly be in this strange place. Jeanette was lying on a cot in a long bare room with practically no furniture besides three other cots exactly like hers. It looked a little like the place where she used to go to summer camp when she was a little girl.

The walls were unadorned . . . no pictures or any other attempt at decoration, and no rugs on the floor. The decor sure wasn't much. Keli would hate it here.

She climbed off her cot. Her legs were wobbly and her head felt as though it might float off. She couldn't seem to think clearly. What had happened and how had she gotten here?

With great effort, she tried to remember. The memory was painful and she had difficulty accepting it. QL47, their good friend, had betrayed them. He'd turned them over to the protectors.

Dimly she could recall being carried along by two of those brown-clad dolts until they reached some sort of shelter. She'd been thirsty, so when they offered her a drink, she'd taken a sip. It had tasted like plain water, but after that she couldn't remember anything. No doubt her drink had been drugged.

Still feeling shaky, she found her way to an open, screened window. What kind of prison was this with windows? She looked out and found herself staring at a wide expanse of blue-green ocean.

She couldn't seem to think clearly. If they'd drugged her for transport to the prison camp, how would she ever find her way back? Then she remembered. Van and QL47 both had said there was no escape from this place. Maybe they were right. Maybe she'd never see Mom and Dad, or even Lillian and Keli again. And Amy! Who would go to her aid now? Nobody. That was the obvious answer.

Feeling sick and miserable, convinced for the first time in her life that any effort she could make would be totally pointless, Jeanette stumbled back to her bed, flopped down, and closed her eyes. She drifted in and out of sleep, seeming to hear voices now and then.

She didn't want to wake up. There was no reason to.

Finally something brushed her hair back from her forehead and touched her face. "She doesn't feel feverish," a woman's voice said.

She opened her eyes. A large, grandmotherly-looking woman was standing over her. "I think it's just the aftereffect of something they gave her."

Jeanette sat up. "I was drugged," she announced.

The grandmotherly woman eyed her calmly. "Everyone's drugged here. It's the way they keep us out of trouble."

"It made me feel awful, like it was the end of the world."

The woman laughed softly. "I've got news for you. That's where you are."

Feeling much more like herself again now that the medication was beginning to wear off, Jeanette took in her surroundings with more observant eyes. As she'd noticed before, there was a window with only a screen over it for protection, and at the far end of the long room, a door stood open.

Two other women were in the room beside the one who still hovered over her. All three were looking at her with a mixture of amusement and concern.

"I remember when I first got here," a small dark-haired woman, who looked to be hardly more than a girl, told the others. "Talk about scared."

"Me too." The other one nodded.

"I'm not scared," Jeanette told them. She wasn't either, not exactly, now that the mind-confusing drug had worn off. Somehow, she'd find the way out.

The other three laughed as though she'd said something funny. "Of course you're not," the large woman agreed, going over to sit on the next cot. She bent to unbuckle her sandals.

It was the first time Jeanette had noticed that clothes were different here. The women were wearing what looked like bathing suits. One wore sandals, the other two were in bare feet.

"I saw the sea."

"That's right. We're on an island."

An island! Jeanette's heart sank, but she recognized the logic of it. It wasn't the first time that an island had been selected as the perfect place for a prison.

"I was with some friends. Do you know if they were brought here?"

The big woman scowled. "If you want to call that machine your friend, you can. But if I were you, I'd keep quiet about it. He sure isn't too popular here."

Jeanette supposed she shouldn't consider him her friend any longer, but it had been obvious that his mind had been adjusted, what would have once been called brainwashing, she supposed. And he'd been very confused about what he'd done.

"Where is this?" she asked.

"We told you. It's an island."

"What's it called?"

Her nearest neighbor shrugged. "Nobody ever told us. I guess it doesn't have a name."

"And what is this building?"

"It's one of the women's dorm rooms."

"And will I be allowed to see my friends?"

The woman laughed. "I sure can see why you're here, honey. You're just full of questions. Don't you know life's much nicer if you don't ask so many?"

Jeanette got up and explored the small building. It didn't take long. There was a sleeping area and a bathroom. She showered quickly and put on her yellow coverall. Thanks to the repellent quality of the cloth the garment still seemed wearable.

Back in the sleeping room, she found the three women standing and waiting for her. "Time to go eat," the small, dark one told her.

They went together to a central dining room where short lines formed at each of the four food dispensers. Jeanette selected soup and a salad and carried the food on a tray to the table where the three women were seated. She kept looking around, hoping to see Neil, Jesse, or QL47, but saw no familiar faces. She did see protectors, half a dozen of them, standing unobtrusively along the walls of the bare, barrackslike dining room.

The food was good and she ate hungrily, listening to the conversation around her but not taking part in it. Finally she caught some reference to the "synthetic monsters."

"You're talking about the protectors?"

"Them and all the guardians." One of her dorm mates spat out the word as though it was repulsive. "We don't like synthetics here."

It was the first real criticism Jeanette had heard of the guardians, other than the things Van had said. And she could see by the expressions of the others at the long table, the nods and the tightened mouths, that they shared a real hatred of the guardians. Was that what brought them here finally? Were they the ones who couldn't accept the guardians, even after reculturing?

A sudden disturbance near the door made her look around. People at the nearest table were throwing bits of food at someone who'd just entered. The newcomer, a man in white coveralls that contrasted with the varied colors the others wore, stood, looking embarrassed. It was QL47!

Jeanette got up, barely conscious that one of the other women grabbed her arm in an attempt at restraint. "Don't go over there." She heard the words dimly but paid no attention to them.

Jesse and Neil were with QL47, one walking on either side of him as though to offer him their support. It was odd, Jeanette thought, that none of the protectors interfered in any way. It was as though nothing out of the ordinary was going on.

Neil spotted her and hurried forward. She couldn't refrain from grabbing him and giving him a little shake. It was better, she knew, than hugging him. He would have died from shame at being publicly hugged by his sister.

"We've been so worried about you," she scolded.

He grinned. "Jesse's been filling me in on what you two have been up to. It's no fair. You got to have all the fun while I was locked up."

The disturbance from the crowd was increasing. Several men had gotten up to go over and exchange words with QL47, and one or two had even aimed a punch in his direction. QL47 just stood there without resistance, though Jesse had doubled his own fists. It wasn't until he and one of the hecklers were about to exchange blows that the protectors intervened.

"They don't care what people do to QL47," Neil said angrily. "But they won't let one of us get hurt. It goes against their code or something."

"Perhaps we'd better leave," Jeanette suggested, leading the way across to where QL47 and Jesse waited.

"We left at breakfast without eating, but we can't keep doing that. We'll starve."

"I've already eaten. Why don't I take QL47 outside while you and Jesse grab some food."

"Okay, we'll meet you down at the beach."

In spite of his obvious fury, Jesse looked at her searchingly, as if to make sure she was okay. "We were worried when you didn't show up for breakfast, but nobody would tell us a thing."

"I had trouble waking up from the drugs. Anyway, right now I'm going to take QL47 down to the beach."

It wasn't until they were outside in the sunshine that Jeanette realized how strange it was that they were all looking after QL47. By rights they should be furious with him. He had betrayed them to the guardians. But they all, even Jesse who'd been so angry at first, seemed to have come to an acceptance that something was very wrong with their friend.

"Lucky you don't need to eat," she told him cheerfully as they strolled away from the dining hall.

"Fortunate indeed since my presence is so disturbing to everyone here." His voice still sounded thin and ill, very unlike his previously authoritative tone. "My power supply should last for centuries, in fact."

He didn't look at her, but stared out at the rolling sea. Jeanette didn't know what to say. "Why did the guardians send you here?"

"I am defective. They can't trust me anymore."

She hated to say the obvious, but they hadn't time for playing games. "Then it seems to me the logical thing for them to have done would have been to dismantle you. Obviously this is where they send *people* they consider defective, not guardians."

"Normally I would have been disassembled and my spare parts put to use, but I was sent here because of you, Jesse, and Neil."

Jeanette frowned. "I don't understand."

"The keeper is important. I was sent here to watch the keeper." He sounded like a small child reciting lines carefully memorized.

"You mean you're to spy on us?"

"For your own good, of course," he assured her.

"Oh, of course," she returned wearily.

They didn't talk anymore as they strolled on down to where waves lapped at the sandy beach. Jeanette turned to look back at the camp itself. It was composed of the large central dining hall from which they'd just come, several other buildings of approximately the same size, and perhaps fifty of the smaller dormitory units. All were built from the same weathered wood. "It does look like a camp," she said.

"It was so designed. A simple, uncluttered life, with adequate food, exercise, and intellectual stimulation seemed the best answer for disturbed minds."

Jeanette felt like saying that most of the minds she'd met so far had seemed less disturbed than angry. They were just plain mad at the guardians! But maybe, in this society, that was the ultimate insanity.

"It's not a very big place."

"No, reculturing is quite successful in the majority of cases. Fortunately this extreme remedy is rarely necessary."

"I suppose it is unusual to find such desperate criminals as you and me," she said, intending sarcasm. She was annoyed when he nodded solemnly. "QL47, we've got to get out of here."

"That would not be in your best interest."

"Seems like I've heard that before." She sank dejectedly down on the sand and began absentmindedly sifting the warm, golden grains through her fingers. Obviously QL47 wasn't going to be much help this time. The stress of trying to perform his programmed mission, with Jeanette and the others pulling him one way and his fellow guardians the opposite, had been too much. His mind *was* disturbed.

She looked up at him thoughtfully. The guardians planned to use him against them, so they had to be careful what they said around him. But there was no reason he couldn't be helpful to them as well. "QL47, you once said you'd answer my questions truthfully."

"To the best of my knowledge, I have always done so, Jeanette."

"Did the guardians tell you to keep certain information from us? Are there restricted areas you're not supposed to talk about?"

"They mentioned no secret areas. After all, you can't leave the prison camp so what harm can you do?"

It was not a comforting idea that the guardians were so secure in this confinement area that they weren't even worried about the possibility of escape.

"The women in my dorm said we were on an island. Is that right?"

"It is an island."

"How large is it?"

"Two and a quarter miles across, about ten miles long."

"Any buildings on it other than the ones we see here?"

"Yes, the central authority buildings are on the other side."

"Central authority?"

"That's where food and other supplies are

brought in and where hopeless cases are finally resolved. But I don't like to think about that."

He sounded so upset that she was puzzled, but it didn't seem a good time to pursue the matter further. She didn't want him so rattled he couldn't give out information.

"How do they get the supplies to the island? Transporter tube?"

"There are no tubes to the prison island. Supplies are brought in by air."

Air! That meant planes or helicopters or something of the sort. And when they came in, the possibility of hiding inside the vehicle and getting away had to exist. "Where do the planes land, QL47? Is there an airstrip near that central building?"

He looked down to frown at her. "No one lands. The supplies are dropped to the ground, the fall conditioned by chutes."

She stared at him in dismay, still groping for hope. "But the guardians, how do they leave? I know they're here because I saw protectors in the dining hall."

He nodded. "Other guardians too."

"And how do they return to the city?"

He shook his head. "Guardians never leave prison island. When their power sources fade, they are simply replaced."

"Dropped just like the supplies?"

"That is correct."

Jeanette got up and went over to the water's edge. This was an attractive place to live: water, everything taken care of, no problems. She even had her friends here.

Angry with her own thoughts, she stomped back to where QL47 still stood. "You needn't think I'm giving up," she snapped.

"I never thought that, Jeanette, but to me it seems quite impossible."

He sounded so sad that she was taken aback. "You make it seem like you want us to escape."

"Not if it's not what's best for you and the guardians say—" He stopped abruptly. "I was so sure before, Jeanette, but now that we're all together again, I'm beginning to wonder."

"Can't you just think for yourself?" She couldn't help being annoyed; this kind of logic was what had gotten them in this mess.

"I'm not supposed to. My thought processes have all been carefully programmed, but Jeanette, I am beginning to wonder."

He'd said that before. She stared curiously at him. "Maybe that's a healthy sign."

"Perhaps." He leaned closer to her. "But let's be careful where we talk. Some areas contain listening devices."

"You mean they're bugged!"

He shook his head, looking puzzled. "No, they're quite insect free. Precautions are taken."

She laughed. "It doesn't matter anyway, QL47, we know that you're in constant communication with the guardians anyway. They know your every thought."

"Not anymore. Not since I broke that communication force to help you and the boys escape. That's why I'm defective. I don't fit in anymore. I don't connect."

He sounded so disconcerted that she was startled. "Then you have to think for yourself. You have no other choice."

"But the guardians have been telling me what to think. It's most comforting."

"It's the easy way, QL47, but not the best way. You must learn to depend on your own thinking."

"Sometimes, Jeanette, it seems it would be better if I just walked into the sea and let the water gradually erode my electronic abilities. It probably wouldn't take more than a hundred years or so."

It took a minute for Jeanette to understand what he was talking about. Finally she began to grasp. "You mean you'd destroy yourself?"

He nodded glumly. "Everyone would be better off."

In sudden alarm, Jeanette grabbed his arm. "We wouldn't be better off, QL47. We'd miss you terribly."

"But I'm the one who arranged your capture. You didn't want to be taken prisoner."

"That's true and I'm still mad at you about it, but that doesn't mean I want you to do anything drastic. I still like having you around."

"You do, Jeanette?" His tone was considerably stronger than it had been at the beginning of the conversation.

She nodded, glancing back toward the buildings. "I can't imagine what's keeping Jesse and Neil. They were supposed to pick up some food and come out here to join us."

"Shall we go look for them?"

Jeanette considered, then shook her head.

"Let's wait another minute or two. We don't want to start a riot by taking you back in there."

"They hate me."

"They hate the guardians. They don't know you're different."

"I am different, Jeanette."

"And that's good, QL47," she said fiercely. "That's good."

She couldn't help being worried about the two boys. Why didn't they come out? But she didn't want QL47 to get concerned and go charging into the dining hall looking for them. He definitely wasn't in a mental state to face that hostile crowd. She tried to think of something to keep his mind occupied. He seemed to like answering questions.

"They drugged us before we were brought here, didn't they? Was that so we couldn't find our way back?"

"They didn't want you to be afraid of the air trip."

"Why would we be afraid of a little flight?"

"Not the flight, the drop."

Jeanette tried to keep him from seeing that she was watching the door of the dining hall. No one was coming out. Something must be going on in there. "You mean they dropped us the way they drop supplies? Sounds like that would hurt." She rubbed her shoulder thoughtfully as though searching for possible injuries.

"Oh, no, they take every precaution and are very careful. It is the most basic element of any guardian's programming that human beings must not be allowed to be injured."

"Then how do they manage it? The drop, I mean."

"Cushioning devices and chutes. It's not that complicated. Perhaps you'd like to watch the next one come in."

"Could we? Would they let us?"

"Of course, I told you there are no secrets on prison island. I'll simply ask that we be notified the next time a delivery is due to arrive."

"That'd be really interesting," Jeanette assured him. Finally, someone was coming out the door from the dining hall. It was Neil, and Jesse was just behind him.

Jeanette was able to breathe more easily at the sight of them, striding along toward her. "Here come Jesse and Neil. They must have eaten in the hall because they're not carrying anything." She frowned. "What's wrong with Neil's face?"

It wasn't until her brother came a little closer that Jeanette was able to answer her own question. "He has something white smeared all over his face."

"Jesse's face is also adorned," QL47 observed.

"What happened?" Jeanette asked as the two boys came up to them.

Jesse looked a little embarrassed. "We had a disagreement with some of the folks in there."

Jeanette touched the substance on her brother's face. "What is this stuff?"

"Mashed potatoes," he admitted sheepishly. "I got a whole plateful right in the face."

"Mine is ripe tomato." Jesse wiped the red

stuff from around his eyes. "Seems we aren't real popular around here."

"It is entirely my fault," QL47 said mournfully.

"Oh, no," Jeanette protested.

Neither of the boys said anything. She glared meaningfully at them.

"He did turn you in to the guardians," Neil pointed out.

"It was a mistake," QL47 agreed, "I was confused. But now that I'm more myself again, I will be able to help you. In fact, Jeanette, I'll go right now and see if I can get that information you want."

The three drew closer together as they watched him walk away. "Where's he going?" Neil asked suspiciously.

"Probably to the central authority building. He's going to find out when the next drop is planned so we can watch."

"Drop?" Neil looked at her as though her sanity was in question.

"QL47 tells me that everything—supplies, guardians, and people—are dropped here on the island. We're virtually cut off from the outside world."

"Dropped?" Neil sounded irritated.

"From the air."

"Wouldn't that hurt?"

"He says they have cushioning devices and some kind of parachute. This is the future, Neil. They've probably developed something new and I want to see what it is. So QL47 is going to find out when the next drop will be made and we'll watch."

"If he's right, Jeanette, this is going to make it hard for us to get away." Jesse's drawl was at its most thoughtful.

She nodded, their eyes meeting. "But we have to get away. We have to help Amy."

"But if they know when a drop is coming, it means they do have communications out of here at least," Neil said excitedly. "Maybe we can steal a radio or something."

"The guardians are communication devices themselves. But even if we had a radio, what good would it do? We don't know anybody to call for help."

"That's true." Neil sank down on to the sand, his enthusiasm gone.

They left him sitting there, staring out to sea as though he could force a rescue boat to materialize for them. As they strolled along the water's edge, they kept their distance from the other people on the beach.

"It's because of QL47 that nobody wants to have anything to do with us, isn't it?"

Jesse nodded. "They hate the guardians here. Can't much blame them, I guess."

"But QL47's different. Can't they see that?"

"Jeanette, I reckon he is, but don't forget that they were able to make him do what they wanted. Don't trust him too far."

In spite of herself, Jeanette knew he was right. "He says he's been disconnected from that mental linkage all guardians have. He's an outcast because of us."

"If it's true. You can't just accept it because that's what he said."

She wanted to argue, but she looked up to meet his eyes, then nodded. "I keep thinking of the aliens being shot down from the sky and here we are doing nothing!"

He took her hand, holding it tightly as though he understood her frustration. "When we get away from here and back to the timeway, we can go there at any time we want just by picturing it in our minds. You know that. So we'll get there to help Amy and the others in plenty of time."

As Jeanette watched a wave roll in, she remembered walking with Amy along another beach. "This time-travel stuff has me mixed up. Whatever's happened to Amy has already taken place. We were there with her when the aliens landed days ago."

"But it hasn't happened yet. It's still more than thirty-five years until they get here."

Jeanette smiled. "But how can that be? How can things be corrected, be changed in past or future? Surely, it's all fixed in place, written so that it can't be rewritten."

Jesse eyed her calmly. "I don't worry a lot about the whys and the wherefores. All I know is that we went there and saw it happening. There's a chance we can improve the situation."

Jeanette laughed. "That's practical, but I can't help thinking and figuring."

"That's the kind of mind you have. Nothing wrong with that."

"But time, Jesse, how can it be something you can move through as though you were walking through a maze?"

"The way I see it, we move through time a second, a minute, a day at a step. But somehow, with this timeway thing, we're able to cut across, to step backward and forward."

"And nothing is fixed, nothing is certain. That's what QL47 said." Jeanette felt as though a door had just been opened a little so that she could begin to see what lay beyond. "We can affect everything and, somehow, we have to change that day in two thousand ninety-nine. But how, Jesse?"

He shook his head. "I wish I knew."

They were startled from their concentration by a shout behind them. QL47 was running toward them.

CHAPTER SIX

"He runs real fast when he puts his mind to it," Jesse observed with a detachment that Jeanette couldn't help envying.

"What's wrong, QL47?" Jeanette called. She saw Neil jump up and follow after their mechanical friend, his shorter flesh-and-blood body unable to begin to keep pace. She gripped Jesse's hand more tightly as the white-clad figure came up to them.

He didn't wait for Neil's arrival before beginning to talk. "It's now, Jeanette. We must hurry."

He turned and would have run off, expecting them to follow. Jeanette was prepared to do so, but Jesse wouldn't release her hand. He stood stubbornly holding her in place.

"Just a minute here. Hold your horses. What's this all about, QL47?"

"The drop. Jeanette wanted to see the next

drop and it's due to happen within minutes. We have to hurry to the other side of the island."

This was enough explanation for Jeanette. She tried to take off, dragging Jesse with her. But Jesse was too big to be dragged.

"What if this is another trap?"

"Come on, Jesse. They've got us already. We're in prison. What else can they do to us?"

"I suppose you're right. Let's go, QL47."

The guardian nodded, then started running, Jeanette and Jesse following. Jeanette was conscious of startled looks from the people around them who cleared a pathway, as though the other prisoners were fearful that an insane guardian was on the loose. As they passed Neil, he fell into step behind them. "What's going on?" he yelled.

"We're on our way to see a drop," Jeanette yelled back. "QL47 says one is coming in now."

They ran past the cluster of buildings where the prisoners lived and into an area of tropical growth. Mentally Jeanette catalogued the greenery for escape possibilities but decided that the sapling-slender trees would be of little value in building a raft or a boat even if they had time for such activities.

The island was not a large one, but enough distance had to be covered to make them slow down to a walk before they broke into a run again. Jeanette caught a glimpse of the sea and heard the pounding of the surf. She barely had time to take in the appearance of a spreading complex of buildings that was totally different in style from the camp on the other side of the island. The buildings were functional, made of some dully gray material and were reminiscent of the structures in the guardian city.

"Now!" QL47 shouted.

Still gasping for breath, Jeanette turned to him.

QL47 pointed upward. "It's coming."

In the midst of a cloudless blue sky hovered a small, sleek airplane. It didn't look that much different from the speedy jets of Jeanette's world, it was entirely silent.

She was about to ask QL47 about that silence when her attention was diverted by an object falling from the plane. At first it fell straight down, dropping as though it were a metallic egg laid by the plane. Then a soft lavender chute ballooned out around the object, which drifted gently toward the island. The plane flew on, headed toward the distant horizon now that its mission was accomplished.

The object drifted purposefully toward an area behind the building complex. "I wish we could see it land."

"We can." QL47 strode toward the complex.

Jeanette raced to keep up with him. "Won't the guardians mind us nosing around here?"

He shook his head. "No secrets," he reminded her.

He led them around to a grassy field that stretched behind the buildings.

"We could make a great football field here," Neil said.

No one paid any attention to him. Jeanette, uncomfortably conscious of two protectors looming at the far end of the field, moved closer to Jesse's side. "Maybe we'd better go back."

Jesse seemed to consider. "They're not paying any attention to us so apparently QL47 is right and they don't care."

"Certainly my statement was correct." QL47 sounded quite human in his indignation. "The people on this island are different. They're curious about things. That, of course, is one of the character defects that caused them to be sent here. Anyway, the guardians try to be open about their activities and allow the humans to view whatever they like. Strangely enough, I'm told, after a few weeks they usually keep to themselves."

"They don't much like guardians," Neil told him.

"Apparently not. Odd, isn't it?"

Jeanette grinned. QL47 sounded as though his feelings were a little hurt. It was funny that the longer she knew him, the harder it was to think of him as anything other than a real person.

They watched with interest as a large, flatbedded truck, which had tiny fat tires that only rose a few inches from the ground, moved to the center of the field. On the bed rested a cushioned surface, something like an extremely large mattress with double-thick padding.

As the parachuted object drifted down toward the padding, Jeanette found herself almost unconsciously moving toward the truck. The others followed.

"It's a person!" Neil announced in a whispered exclamation.

Jeanette, who'd been concentrating on the apparent landing site, looked upward. The object was now close enough to the ground for her to see that Neil was right.

The person who dangled at the end of the chute was strapped into something shaped like a canoe, wide in the middle and with ends that sloped upward.

"Is he dead?" she heard Neil ask in a stunned voice. "That looks like a coffin."

"Looks like a canoe to me," she argued.

"The person is not dead," QL47 interjected calmly, "but simply wrapped into a cushioned device for protection during the drop."

They watched as the chute drifted down to the ground so that the figure was lowered gently to the cushioned bed of the truck. "Lucky it landed there."

"Luck has nothing to do with it," QL47 assured her. "The drop is carefully calculated."

"I'll bet they miss sometimes," Neil said.

"Is this how we were brought here?" Jesse asked.

"Of course." QL47 nodded. "I was conscious and aware of what was going on, but you were unconscious."

"Drugged!" Jeanette said in disgust.

The protectors hurried to remove the rather small figure of the latest newcomer to prison island from the cushions. Jeanette drew closer to observe the procedure, then grabbed Jesse's arm. "It's Van."

The boy stretched out before them looked small

and limp, his face pale and his eyes closed. She couldn't help wondering if he was all right.

"I warned Van Lee," QL47 said. "He'd run out of time. The guardians lost patience with him."

"You sound pleased, QL47."

"Well, Jeanette, he was a thoroughly unpleasant boy."

"Why do you say 'he was'? He is going to be all right, isn't he?"

QL47 didn't answer directly. Instead he shook his head. "Such a shame. He had so many natural gifts."

"But he might grow up to fill an important role." Jeanette clutched desperately at the arguments she'd used to get QL47 to help them escape last fall. "Did you check his life history?"

QL47 nodded. "Of course. I was his first tutor and I'm quite thorough about such things. He was born in nineteen ninety-two, lived his first six years in a normal enough fashion, then vanished."

"But his family must have searched for him? How terrible for them."

"Fortunately he had no close relatives still living at the time of his departure. Don't worry about that."

"But did you look into the future? Maybe he never went back, but just went on from here."

"I've told you before, Jeanette, time isn't set in fixed patterns. It isn't as though each person simply walks through a pre-established life. Choices are made and lives change because of those choices. In Van Lee's case, the possibilities were discouraging. One of the ways he could have gone, the most likely in fact, would have led him into becoming a rebellious young man and finally a petty dictator. His political career could only have been brief, however; his understanding of people was limited. He would have had a very thin base of power with no true support."

Jeanette closed her eyes for a second, confused between past and present. "But he's only eight years old and you talk as though his life was already over. You can't let them kill him."

"Kill!" QL47 looked shocked. "Certainly not." He shook his head sadly. "But just the same, life is over for Van Lee."

He insisted they leave. No argument would convince him they should stay longer. And when the protectors began to move somewhat ominously toward them, Jeanette allowed herself to be persuaded.

It was getting late by the time they got back to the camp area and Jeanette realized dejectedly that she was no closer to having an escape plan than when the day began.

That night they ate together in the dining hall, insisting that QL47 accompany them even though he didn't consume food. They found themselves allotted an isolated corner table in an area of the room noticeably avoided by the other diners, but nobody threw food this time or made insulting remarks.

After dinner they walked through the compound together and saw Van Lee brought into one of the dorms on a stretcher carried by two protectors. He was still asleep.

QL47 watched with an air of intellectual interest. "So they're not going to do it right away," he said. "I suppose they're making an example of him. A public occasion."

It made Jeanette shiver to hear him talk this way, but he wouldn't elaborate, not even when she insisted. "I may be wrong. I'm not sure what the guardians have in mind for him."

She wondered if he realized that he was beginning to speak of the guardians as though he were not one of them.

"We've got to do something," Neil said. "You can't let them hurt an innocent little kid like that."

Jeanette, Jesse, and QL47 all stared at him. "Just wait until you meet Van," Jeanette said, managing to laugh. "Just wait."

Neil met Van the next morning at breakfast. The four of them were seated at the same table they'd had the night before, eating one of the big country meals that Jesse preferred, when Neil nudged his sister. "Isn't that your friend?"

Jeanette looked up. It was Van, standing in the doorway, surveying the situation with a practiced eye. "Who wants to bet that he'll pretend not to see us? We're not his favorite people."

"Young Mr. Lee doesn't like anybody other than himself," QL47 said.

"I'm not so sure," Jesse disagreed.

Van did see them, Jeanette was sure of it. His eyes narrowed as he looked their way. He started over, only to be stopped by one of the women from Jeanette's dorm, who talked rapidly, looking straight at QL47 as she spoke.

"Now he sure won't remember us," Jeanette said, "not with Elissa filling him in on our status here."

"Are they giving you a rough time at your bunkhouse?" Neil asked.

"Not exactly. They just pretend I'm not there."

He sighed. "That's better than the deal Jesse and I've got. As far as QL47 is concerned, he spent the night on the beach."

"I didn't mind. It was a lovely night."

Jeanette was more than a little surprised when Van, having listened intently to Elissa's information, nodded politely to her, then headed directly toward them.

"Hi, Jeanette, Jesse," he said. "Guess I didn't do you any big favor by helping you get together with this guy." His nod indicated QL47.

"No big favor, Van Lee," QL47 agreed. "I turned them over to the protectors. No malice was intended, however, it seemed the best thing to do at the time."

Van pulled out a chair and sat down. "You guys really get me. All this big-deal talk about what's good for everybody. You're really in it for what's good for you."

Jeanette sipped her orange juice. It was nice to know that some things didn't change. One of those was the obnoxious personality of Van Lee. "Give him credit, Van. He means it. He got the worst end of the deal anyway. He got sent here where everybody hates him."

"I grasped that. That woman." He pointed at

Elissa. "Told me to stay away from you. She said the synthetic monster has you under his influence and you can't think for yourselves. The way she talked, I thought I might catch it if I got too close."

"What nonsense!" QL47 snapped. "Have you had anything to eat yet, Van?"

The sudden switch in topics made the boy blink. Then he shook his head. "I'm not hungry."

"You need food. It will counteract the effect of the drug. We certainly don't want you operating with a muddled brain."

QL47 got up to march in the direction of the nearest food dispenser. At his approach, the people in line scattered to stare at him from a distance while he calmly selected food items.

"What gets me is why you're still hanging around with him if he's such a traitor," Van said.

"He was confused. They reprogrammed him to think he'd been wrong to help us before. They convinced him that turning us in was the best thing he could do for us."

"Still, I'd think you'd be a little mad."

"We're taking nothing for granted," Jesse assured him, "but right now we seem to be in this thing together. We're trying to find a way to escape."

"Can't be done." Van looked smug. "Not by anyone with only a normal brain."

"Hey!" Neil protested. "Jesse's smart as anyone."

It was as if Van saw the other boy for the first time. He considered him thoughtfully, then turned back to the other two as though finding him too insignificant for further attention. "No offense, Jesse. It's only that in the whole history of this place, nobody's ever gotten away. It isn't a challenge I would have chosen, but now that I'm here I'm ready to take it on."

"You mean you think you can escape, a little kid like you?" Neil asked incredulously.

"I already have a plan in mind. Just going to take me a few days to get it going."

Van was unaware that QL47 had come up behind him and jumped when a tray of food was placed before him. "A few days may be too long, Van Lee. You may not have that much time left."

Van paled as though he knew what QL47 was talking about. For a moment he looked frightened, but seconds later he was digging into his breakfast like any ordinary hungry boy.

Neil still regarded him suspiciously. "You really think you're a smart kid, don't you?"

Van looked up at the other boy. "I *am* smart. Why go around acting like I don't know it?"

"People might like you better. Besides, you might find you're not as smart as you think. If you were really that brilliant, you wouldn't have ended up here."

"I notice you're here too."

Neil got up, slammed his dishes into the disposer, and stalked out of the dining hall.

"Neil seems a bit tense," QL47 observed.

"Don't know why he would be. He's only locked up here for the rest of his life." Jeanette stared at the remains of her breakfast. "Truth is that he's been acting strange for quite a while now. He's got this idea that he's going to be the keeper and the responsibility weighs him down."

QL47 looked thoughtfully in the direction Neil had gone. "The future still writes itself, but the probability is great that Neil will play a highly significant role in it."

"The future? But from your viewpoint, we come from the past. You can just look in the history books to learn what's become of any of us."

"It is there. But I told you before, everything is subject to change. An action on one end of history can be reflected in many other changes."

This made Jeanette think of something. "I know one change that just didn't make sense. After you sent us home, QL47, Jesse ended up back in the past of our world, not his own."

QL47 nodded. "That's because I was unable to complete either my directions or the coordinates."

"But at first he couldn't make the timeway work, then suddenly, for no reason, it did work, and he ended up on the unicorn ride at the carnival in our time. How do you explain that?"

QL47 studied her face thoughtfully. "The guardians froze the timeways behind you. You were never supposed to be able to access it again. Apparently some action caused matters to change."

"But nobody did anything," Jeanette protested. "Amy and I had ridden on the unicorn timeway, but that didn't have anything to do with Jesse."

"Perhaps not, but it is possible that something you did caused a wavering along the pathways of time that reached out to affect Jesse. As I said, each action causes a variety of reactions."

"That's enough to make a person scared to move for fear he's going to upset everything," Jesse said.

"It should be enough to make us proceed very cautiously when it comes to dealing with the timeway," QL47 agreed. "That's why after the first open years of experiment, the guardians decided to be highly selective about who could travel in time. The havoc that resulted from those early years is only now beginning to be put under control."

"You think we should use the timeways?" Jesse leaned back in his chair to regard QL47 thoughtfully.

"I know the results if you do not travel. The worst possibilities will occur."

"You said the time principle wouldn't be discovered and there would be terrible wars."

He nodded. "That is true, but by now you have moved far enough along the road. The pathway to the discoveries of the keeper is clear now."

Jeanette shook her head. "I can't see what's happened that makes you say that."

"The process has begun. It is under way."

"But what about Amy and her people?"

He sighed. "It is hard to see that future now. All I know is that without you, they will die."

"Who cares about a bunch of people we don't even know," Van said with pointed rudeness.

"Right now the one I'm worried about is me. How long do I have, QL47?"

"Not long. But I am no longer in the confidence of the guardians. I do not know their specific plans."

The boy nodded as though whatever it was that QL47 referred to no longer scared him. "Then I won't take any chances."

He got up, leaving his tray on the table. "I've got to go take care of something," he said before leaving the table with no further goodbye.

Jeanette looked questioningly at QL47. "What's going on? What is it that you think is going to happen to Van?"

He shook his head and got up to follow the boy.

Jeanette felt a touch on her hand and looked up to smile at Jesse. "How are we going to get away from here?" she asked, feeling really down for once. The way out just didn't seem to exist. "It looks hopeless."

He gave her hand a comforting little pat. "I'm going to have a long talk with Van. There's a good chance he knows more than he's telling and he can help us escape."

"Van? Oh, he just likes to boast."

Jesse shook his head. "It's more than that. Like he knows a secret or something. I'm going to find out. Maybe he can help us."

"As if he would!"

"I'll be real persuasive." She felt comforted by his familiar grin. "I'll have to convince him that he'll be better off if he takes us along."

Jeanette couldn't quite believe that an eight-year-old boy, no matter how brilliant, could be their answer to getting off the island. "You really think he's got a plan?"

He gave her hand another pat. "I'm sure he has. He'll put it into action in the next few hours. Something about what QL47 said scared him good, and I've got a feeling he's not going to stand around waiting. And we don't want to be left behind."

They left the dining hall together, but Jesse went off to look for Van and Jeanette headed in the opposite direction.

CHAPTER SEVEN

Jeanette spent the morning alone on the far end of the beach trying to think up a plan of her own. But by noon, she had to admit she wasn't getting anywhere and headed back to the dining hall. She wasn't particularly hungry, but she did hope she'd run into the others there.

She waited an hour, nibbling at a chicken-salad sandwich that was almost as good as the ones Lillian made. No one showed up. Grumpily, she wondered if they'd all gotten together somewhere without her and were at work executing Van's plan.

Not QL47, she corrected mentally. Van would never trust any guardian enough to let him in on secret plans, particularly not now that he knew they'd been betrayed by QL47.

Still she wondered where they were.

They weren't anywhere in sight. Jeanette

couldn't help beginning to worry. She searched through the housing area and asked everyone she met of their whereabouts, but nobody admitted to having seen them. Finally, she started down the beach, moving along at a brisk pace.

She found Jesse and Neil only after she walked more than two miles. They were alone and busily engaged in tying together two skinny tree trunks that they'd obviously just hacked down.

"What are you doing?"

Neil grinned. "Playing Huck Finn. Thought we'd go rafting across the ocean."

Jeanette pushed at the two small logs with the toe of her shoe. The vine that the boys had used to tie them together broke and they rolled apart.

"Hey! Be careful," Neil yelled.

"Doesn't much matter," Jesse said disgustedly. "If it's no stronger than that, we sure don't want to go out on the water with it."

"It's a rather small raft anyway," Jeanette teased.

"We were only getting started," her brother told her.

"But it's taken us all afternoon," Jesse added. "The trees on this island are only a few inches around and they're tough as iron. It took hours for us to even whittle one down with a knife from the dining hall."

"Plastic," Neil reminded her, "but a tougher kind than the ones Mom buys for picnics."

"Still not much of a cutting tool, but all we had."

"In other words," Jeanette said, "at this rate

it's going to take us a good many years to get off the island."

Jesse nodded. "If we don't come up with a better idea."

"I gather that Van wasn't much help."

"What did you expect?" Neil asked. "That kid isn't about to help anybody."

"Still, I feel sure he does have a plan, and knowing Van, it probably is something fairly practical. He has that kind of mind." Jesse's expression was thoughtful.

Neil stood up, looking challengingly at Jesse. "If he could think something up, so can we."

Jesse shook his head. "It's not quite that simple. He had more time to prepare. He realized they were after him and that there was at least a possibility he'd end up here. He had a fair idea what this place was like and we hardly even were aware it existed. All we knew was there was a prison colony."

"So Van had more time to think up a plan, is that what you're saying?"

"Something like that." Jesse shrugged as though he wasn't sure what he thought. "Though he could be bluffing."

"I'm sure he is." Neil went back to work, trying to tie the logs together with another piece of vine.

Jeanette couldn't help looking doubtfully at the whole project, feeling quite certain she didn't want to be out on the tossing waves in such a ramshackle contraption.

"Where's QL47?" she asked.

Both boys shook their heads. "Haven't seen him since breakfast," Jesse answered.

Jeanette glanced back down the beach. "I hope he isn't in some kind of trouble."

"What trouble? He knows his way around heaps better than we do," Neil told her. "The whole layout was built into his guardian brain."

"Part of his programming," she corrected. "And he wants to help us."

"That's what he says anyway." Jesse stood up, wiping sweat from his brow.

It was odd, Jeanette thought, the way Jesse came to Van's defense every time and remained distrustful of QL47. "You don't like him, do you?"

"I've got nothing against him. He saved our bacon last fall and I don't forget a favor easy."

"But from the first, you didn't really like him."

He plunged one hand into the pocket of his light blue coveralls, looking a little uncomfortable. "I'm not even used to the machines you have back where you live: cars, washing machines, computers. And people machines really make me feel odd. I don't like being around them."

"Oh, QL47's just some sort of advanced computer on legs," Neil assured him.

"He's more than that," Jeanette said. "He has personality."

"Some people talk to their cars," her brother said indulgently. "Even give 'em names."

Jeanette looked down the beach and saw a speck moving toward them. "Someone's coming."

Hurriedly Neil and Jesse dragged their makeshift raft off the beach and into the covering shrubbery. Jeanette watched the jogging figure draw closer. "You didn't have to hide your stuff. It's only QL47."

She felt a touch on her arm and looked up to see Jesse just behind her. "I'd rather you didn't say anything about the raft to him."

After a minute, she nodded. She didn't like it, but he was right. QL47 might be anxious to help, but the extent to which he could throw off the influence of his fellow guardians still remained to be proven.

QL47 stepped up his speed and within minutes drew up in front of them. He wasn't even breathing hard after the long run. "I thought you'd want to know. They're going to do it tonight." He shook his head. "I know all the old arguments, but I tried to tell them it wasn't the right way. I tried to tell them, but they wouldn't listen."

Jeanette had never seen him so upset. His cool, rational approach to life seemed totally gone. "What is it?" she asked gently. "What's wrong?"

"Van Lee. They're going to take him tonight."

"Take him where?"

"To the web. He's to be placed in a dormant state."

Jeanette stared at him, trying to take it in.

"Dormant, QL47?" Neil asked. "You mean like a caterpillar, or something like that."

"Not exactly. That creature returns in a new form. Van will be kept in a state of being barely alive."

Jeanette still stared, feeling horror. "Why would they do that to him?"

"It is the final step for those who cannot be made to fit in. They say Van Lee will never be happy and that the force of his personality is such that he will make everyone around him unhappy as well. They say it is best to use the web."

Jeanette's mouth was so dry she was sure she couldn't even speak.

"You keep saying 'they.' " Jesse's tone was sharpened with suspicion. "How come you know what the guardians are up to?"

QL47 shook his head very slowly. "It's quite strange. I'm disconnected, but still I receive intermittent messages, fragments of the communications between the guardians."

"Then how do you know you're not sending as well, giving them information about us?"

The gray eyes of the guardian widened with shock. "I can't be sure that's not happening. But Jesse, I don't know any secret information. I can't have given anything away."

Jesse just stood there, looking down at the sand as though he didn't know what to say.

To Jeanette this particular argument seemed pointless when Van was in such big trouble. "You said you talked to the guardians about Van?"

QL47 nodded. "I am able to communicate when I choose. I told them they were wrong to put the boy in the web. That they should give him another chance."

"I thought you didn't like him."

"Not much. I can't feel the same warmth toward him that I do for the three of you. It is difficult to like Van Lee," he added a little apologetically.

Jeanette couldn't argue that point. "We've got to warn him. Let's head back to the camp."

It seemed to Jeanette as they jogged along the beach together that she was always running somewhere these days—something important was usually at stake. This time it was Van Lee's life, and from what QL47 said, it sounded as though the web was even worse than death. His life was simply to be suspended, kept on hold indefinitely.

"Do they ever wake them up from this dormant stage?" she asked.

"Never."

"Then why do it? Why not simply execute him if that's what it amounts to?"

"The guardians were programmed with a great reluctance to cause the death of any human."

"So this is how they get around it. They don't kill. They just keep him from being alive."

"Yes, and he will have a much longer life. Aging takes place in the web, but only at a very slow rate."

Jeanette nodded. She was panting too hard to say anything else. When they got back to the camp, they agreed to separate, hoping that one of them would find the boy quickly. Jesse was to go to the dorm where Van lived, Neil to the dining hall, QL47 would scout the beach in the opposite direction from which they'd just come, and Jeanette would search the woods that lay on the other side, between the camp and the authority complex.

The wooded area was not a popular spot with residents who preferred the beach, so Jeanette encountered only one couple who wanted to be alone and looked at her as though she was intruding when she came dashing through the tropical wood. She smiled apologetically and went on; the urgency of finding Van immediately drove her to run even though the entangling vines threatened to trip her and the thorns tore at her clothing and hair.

Finally she grew desperate. "Van!" she shouted. "Van, where are you?"

No answer. She stopped, feeling that this part of the search was futile. The wood stretched through the entire midsection of the island. The only hope was that one of the others had found him. She might as well go back. *"Van!"* She gave one last, loud shout, not really expecting a response.

The reply came from quite close at hand. "What do you want, Jeanette?"

She found him in a small clearing only a few feet away and stopped to regard him crossly. "Didn't you hear me calling?"

"I heard, but I was busy and didn't really want to be bothered."

"What were you doing that was so involving?"

"Oh, something important."

He had a number of things scattered around him. She bent to look more closely at the items, which she didn't recognize. She picked one small packet up to examine it more closely. "What's this?"

"Fruit juice. These are condensed and dehydrated foods."

"Where did you get them?"

"Out of the dispenser, of course. Look, Jeanette, now that you're here, I want to talk to you about something."

"What's that?"

"Why I can't take you and Jesse with me. I'm really sorry because I'd like to, but it would reduce the chances of success. I just can't run that risk."

Jeanette couldn't help laughing. "Don't worry, Van. I never expected your help. In fact, I've come to help you and I'm glad that you're here in the woods because it gives you a better chance of hiding from the guardians."

He shook his head. "Not really. We have a little more privacy here, that's all. The guardians have built-in heat-seeking abilities. They can locate us anytime they want."

"Even here?" Jeanette looked around fearfully at the thick, tropical shrubbery.

"Sure. Anyway, Jeanette, what I wanted to explain was that it's not the escape itself that's the problem. Once we get out of here you and Jesse would be a liability I couldn't afford. Neither of you knows your way around. I tried to tell Jesse that, but I wanted to tell you too."

The only thing that surprised Jeanette was that he was at all troubled. She would have sworn that he didn't have a conscience.

"Jesse's really a great guy, Jeanette. Under

other circumstances I would have liked to grow up to be like him. But the way things are here, well, you've just got to be tough to survive."

She couldn't help being amused. "Bad guys have used that argument for centuries to justify being the way they are."

His eyes narrowed. "You think I'm a bad guy?"

"Not yet, but you're working on it. The thing is you're never going to get a chance either way if you don't let me tell you what's going on."

His attention sharpened abruptly. "What do you mean?"

"QL47 says the guardians are out looking for you now. He says they're going to put you in something called the web."

Van's body stiffened as though he was paralyzed by fright. His face turned white. "When did he tell you this?"

"Just a few minutes ago. He said he tuned in to the thought waves they were sending and even tried to talk them out of it, but they wouldn't budge. So you can see, you've got to find one terrific hiding place, and fast!"

"It wouldn't do any good. They can find me anywhere on the island."

Jeanette grabbed his arm, suddenly frantic. He might be a brat, but he was only a little kid and he didn't deserve this. "We've got to do something."

"You really want to help me," he said in a wondering tone, "even when I just refused to help you."

"We don't have time to talk about that now." She gave him a little shake. "Let's get going."

Van bent down, removed his left shoe, then his sock. He began to peel away flesh-colored tape from the sole of his foot, finally exposing a thin packet. "This is the only answer," he said. "This is the way we'll get away."

"We?"

"Sure. How can I leave you behind when you've come to warn me? I just wish Jesse and your dumb brother were here."

"Can't we look for them?" Jeanette didn't know why she believed this wild story about the little packet he'd had strapped to the bottom of his foot offering a way of escape, but she did.

He shook his head. "Nope." He sounded genuinely regretful. "No time. We'll all be caught if we go looking for them. But I'll take you on the condition that once we get back, you're on your own."

Jeanette nodded agreement. If the only way to escape was to go without the others, then she'd do it—because then she'd be able to find a way to come back for them. It was better than all of them being stuck here. "Let's do it."

"You're thinking you'll be able to come back and save them," he accused. "I know how your mind works."

She grinned acknowledgment.

"Just don't count on any help from me."

"I won't."

"Okay then, let's get started. We need to wait until we have the cover of darkness, but since we don't have any choice we'll collect all the food containers and the water cartons and get going."

She nodded, wondering what he could possibly do with the little packet that would be that spectacular She'd bent to pick up the items scattered around them when a sudden shout made her straighten.

They were surrounded by protectors. It was too late!

"Run, Van!" she shouted, giving him a push that sent him halfway across the clearing. "I'll distract them." She stuck out a foot to send the first of the giant-sized protectors sprawling across the grass and hammered the hardest blows she could at the midsection of the one just behind him.

But it was hopeless. There were too many of them and she was held in place before she had time to strike more than a few blows. Her arms were pinned at her sides.

They had Van too. He stood, his expression stony, his eyes full of terror. Even his lips were pale.

"Van Lee, we have an order that you be webbed," the leader of the protectors announced solemnly. "Public sentence will be carried out this very night."

Jeanette heard someone whimpering protest and then realized it was her own voice. "No," she shouted in a stronger tone. "You can't do this. He's only a boy."

"A very dangerous boy," the leader told her. "Jeanette Lacy, please be more careful about your activities. We would dislike seeing you meet the same fate." He nodded to the two protectors who had hold of her. "Return her to quarters."

"Wait!" Van shouted. "Let me say goodbye to her. She's my friend."

He shook their hands away and they allowed him to approach her. "One last handshake," he said, a sick-looking smile on his lips.

Stunned, she felt his hand take hers, knew that he was pressing the small packet into her palm. She felt his other hand closing her fingers around it. "Tell Jesse I wish I could've been with you two just a little longer." He managed a faint, croaking laugh before they led him away.

Jeanette was forced to go back to her dorm. She was glad to see that nobody else was there. She sank down on her bunk and stared at the object Van had forced into her hand. It appeared to be a small intricately folded piece of vinyl. It certainly didn't look like anything important.

Totally perplexed, she slipped off her shoe and put it inside, then put the shoe back on. It was a good enough hiding place, she decided, for someone who didn't have pockets in her clothes. Then she went outside to go look for the others so she could tell them what had happened.

CHAPTER EIGHT

After talking over what had happened with the boys and QL47, Jeanette went to her quarters to lie quietly on her bed while trying to think of a way to help Van. It seemed hopeless. She couldn't eat dinner, and when she, along with the other prisoners, was herded across the island to the central authority building, she felt the packet Van had given her in her shoe against her foot. If only she knew how to use this thing he'd given her! Maybe it could help him.

She shook her head almost imperceptibly. Probably not. Something about his farewell made her think that he was only handing over to her something for which he had no further use.

That reminded her. She'd been so upset about Van that she had forgotten to tell anyone about the packet. She'd mention it to them the first chance she got.

"Are you okay, Jean?" Neil asked, hovering protectively at her side.

"Nope, but I don't know what to do about it. How can we just go over there and see them do whatever it is they're going to do to Van?"

"Take it easy, Jeanette," Jesse warned in a soft voice. "QL47 says the guardians are real unhappy because you tried to defend Van. He's afraid you're going to get in trouble."

She couldn't worry about that now. She was too concerned about Van. "Can't we do something?" she demanded almost angrily.

"Keep your voice down." Jesse glared. "You act like you want to get in bad with the guardians."

"I don't care about them."

"Well, you'd better care. Don't act stupid."

His use of Van's favorite word was untimely to say the least. Especially right now when Jeanette felt like bashing heads in. "You don't care about Van. All you're concerned about is saving your own skin."

"It's your skin I'm worried about right now. You might use what brains you've got under those pretty curls."

She stopped abruptly, sputtering with anger. "How can you be so condescending, Jesse Lansden?"

"What's wrong with the two of you?" Neil asked, looking from one to the other.

"It's stress," QL47 said firmly. "I realize it's difficult, but you must go through the motions, Jeanette. Believe me when I say there's nothing any of us can do for Van now. It's not fair to try to pressure Jesse into rash action this way."

"I certainly wasn't trying to pressure Jesse," Jeanette said indignantly.

"Couldn't if she wanted to," Jesse added.

Abruptly one of the protectors loomed over them. "Let's get going," he said in a deep, grating voice. "Or we'll be late for the ceremony."

"We wouldn't want that." Jeanette spoke sarcastically.

Jesse took hold of her arm and forced her into motion again. "Keep quiet, you idiot," he whispered.

Jeanette obeyed, though seething inwardly. She was too mad to cry, she told herself, even though tears crept down her cheeks. They couldn't let this happen to Van!

But it seemed there was nothing to be done. At the complex, they were all led into a large circular building and told to sit in bleacherlike seats that lined the walls. "What is this, public entertainment?" she asked.

"Jeanette, keep your mouth closed," Jesse ordered.

She folded her arms and moved as far away from him as possible. She'd never realized Jesse could be so mean.

"How often is this webbing ceremony done?" she heard him ask QL47.

"It's most uncommon. We have many other steps—the reculturing, even the imprisonment. No one likes to see this happen."

"Then why the audience?" Jeanette demanded in an unsteady voice.

"Because, my dear, they feel that those viewing the ceremony are unlikely to rebel in any meaningful way once they're fully aware of the possible results of such actions."

Dimly she was aware that QL47, who prided himself on his cool detachment, had called her "my dear" in such fatherly fashion. She knew she was behaving irrationally, being angry at Jesse and QL47, but they hadn't been there when Van was taken. They didn't know how scared he'd looked.

"We can't do anything about it right now, Jeanette," Jesse whispered.

She looked up into deep brown eyes that seemed as concerned as ever. "Right now?"

He nodded.

She looked across to QL47. "Is the process reversible? Can he be brought back from dormancy?"

"Of course. That was why this was substituted for the death penalty in the first place. If you kill a person for a crime and then find he or she is innocent, you can hardly give that life back. But in this case, you simply restore the person to fully functioning life processes again." He paused to rub his chin thoughtfully. "It's never happened, though."

"The guardians don't make mistakes?" Jesse asked doubtfully.

"Or don't admit them," Jeanette added.

Around them the other prisoners were talking in a low hum. Jeanette saw a few solemn, thoughtful faces, but most acted as though it were some sort of holiday event, an interesting break in the monotonous routine of life on the island.

When a line of protectors marched onto the lowered floor in the center of the room, the hum died away and collectively the audience leaned forward. Two guardians, dressed in the silver gray that seemed to indicate high authority, came in next. Van walked between them.

Jeanette rose in her seat in unconscious protest and was pulled back into place by Jesse. She tried to draw away, but he wrapped one muscular arm around her shoulders and held her there.

She looked back again to where Van stood, looking young and very frightened. His gaze searched the crowd as though trying to find a familiar face. They were near the back, up at the top of the bleachers. He wouldn't see them.

She pretended to relax against Jesse's arm, letting her body go limp as though giving way to emotion. She felt his hold lessen and seized the opportunity to jump up. She didn't say anything, didn't yell out even though she wanted to, but Van saw. He looked straight up at her and a little smile curved his mouth upward.

She looked around, prepared for Jesse's anger, then saw that he was standing at her side. He smiled at her, then bent to her ear to whisper, "Okay, so we're both wood heads."

A protector approached from the aisle, fiercely waving them back into place, and they sank down again. Maybe they were wood heads—Van's choice expression for the people of this place and time—but at least he'd seen that he had friends in the crowd.

It was time, apparently, for the ceremony to

begin. A large tanklike instrument was rolled into center stage as was a tube-shaped container that was made of glass, clear plastic, or some transparent substance. The machine was connected to the container and turned on so that a dull roar reverberated throughout the building.

Van offered no resistance when one of the guardians pressed a flat disk against his forehead. Seconds later, he collapsed in their arms.

"Jesse!" Jeanette whispered in alarm.

He shook his head.

"They've merely rendered him unconscious," QL47 whispered.

The two guardians who wore gray uniforms seemed to be in charge. One of them lifted Van into the transparent container. The roar increased. The gray guardians closed the see-through lid down over Van.

"Can he breathe in that thing?" Jeanette leaned across Jesse to whisper to QL47.

He nodded. "His respiration will be slowed within seconds. All his body functions will be reduced to an absolute minimum as he enters the dormant stage."

Jeanette watched in horror as the machine went to work. Thin filaments like the branches of a spider's web spun into the cylinder in which Van lay, wrapping him about with a silvery gauze that twined delicately around face and form, encasing him in a gradually thickening mass.

Jeanette felt sickened, suffocated just by the sight of it, and hid her face in her hands. She heard the sounds of the people around her and knew that no one in that large auditorium was under the impression that this was fun. They were as horrified as she.

After a while, she looked up again to find the process nearly finished. Van was hardly recognizable. He was coated in several inches of the silvery web.

Finally QL47 reached over to touch her arm. "It's over now. We can go."

She stumbled to her feet and was vaguely conscious that she followed her dazed-looking little brother to the doorway, the crowd pressing against them as the others exited. Nobody talked much. It was a much quieter group than the one that had entered.

Outside the night air was warm and moist. "He felt no pain," QL47 whispered. "Now he will sleep the decades away, only growing older very gradually."

Nobody said anything as they walked back through the darkness toward the camp, the crowd around them almost as silent as they were.

Back at camp, they strolled down toward the beach, not even talking about the need to be together and discuss what had just happened.

"That was the worst thing I've ever been through," Neil declared, kicking at a shell.

"Me too." Jeanette still felt as though she were shaking inside. "I didn't handle it very well."

"You handled it like the feeling, caring person you are," QL47 said firmly, as though to indicate that he didn't want to hear any criticism of Jeanette, not even from her. "It was a difficult situation."

"Especially for Van," Jesse added quietly.

Jeanette nodded. "I couldn't help wishing we'd known him longer. At the last he was really trying. He was going to help me escape."

"He probably didn't even know a way off the island anyway," Neil said dejectedly.

Jeanette halted, bent down to take off her shoe, and brought out the packet Van had given her. "He had a lot of confidence in this small object, whatever it is. He slipped it to me after they captured him."

Neil took it from her. "Doesn't look like much of anything to me. Just some folds of plastic."

"Let me see that," QL47 commanded curtly.

Jeanette handed it to him, then watched as he turned it over and over in his hands examining every speck of it. Finally he opened it up, exposing a little pull tab.

He looked, Jeanette thought, strangely elated. "What is it?" she asked.

"Doesn't look like much of anything to me," her brother said.

"It's a miniature." QL47 breathed the words as though they were supposed to explain everything.

"A miniature what?" Jeanette asked curiously.

Instead of answering, he looked out at the darkened sea. "He was going tonight, undoubtedly waiting for cover of darkness. But surely he thought about food and water. Humans must have those things."

"He had lots of stuff he'd gotten from the dispenser."

QL47's thin eyebrows slid upward. "That's

what gave him away then. They didn't know what he was planning, but they knew some sort of escape was in the works when he selected all those things from the dispenser. Of course, he had to have them." He looked at Jeanette. "Did they pick up the things he'd gathered when they took him in?"

She shrugged. "Not that I noticed. They were too busy dealing with the two of us. Of course, they could have gone back later and cleared up."

"It's worth a chance. Jesse, you and Neil go back to camp and make your presence very evident while Jeanette shows me where Van's cache was left in the woods."

"But why?" Jeanette asked in bewilderment.

"Because you will need supplies for your journey. You are about to make your escape."

It didn't take long to jog back to camp. From there, Jeanette found the way easily enough to the place in the woods where she'd found Van. QL47 gave a little shout of jubilation when he saw the containers still scattered on the ground. "You'll have to eat sparingly, but these will keep you alive until you get to land."

"We're going on a boat?"

QL47 wouldn't answer. He made her help gather up the supplies Van had left and between the two of them they carried everything back, skirting the camp to find their way to the far end of the beach.

"Now, Jeanette, you will return to camp, find the boys, and come back here. Also bring with you some blankets, if you can do so without being noticed."

She lingered long enough to watch as he took the packet out and began to look it over carefully. "A miniature boat," she said in disbelief.

He laughed softly. "You forget the difference in technology from your time to mine, Jeanette. Yes, it's a water craft of a primitive sort. I'd like to have the story of how Van Lee obtained it, but then I've always had considerable confidence in that young man's ingenuity."

Jeanette told herself that she still couldn't believe that small object could increase in size to anything that could carry even one of them. She hurried obediently back to camp and tucked her blankets under her arm right in front of her door mates. It was easy to use their attitude toward her as an excuse. "Since you're all so fond of me, I'll just sleep on the beach tonight."

She stomped out before anyone had a chance to answer. Strolling casually, she walked down toward the beach, looking for Neil and Jesse, but they saw her before she spotted them, jumping out at her from the shadows on the edge of the sand. "How about a walk, you two," she said loudly for the benefit of the listeners. Softly she whispered, "QL47 wants us back on the double."

Neither said anything until they were out of sight of the camp. "What are the blankets for?" Neil asked. "Don't tell me QL47 got cold."

"He told me to bring them. He said we'd need them on the boat."

"Boat! What boat?"

Jeanette was reluctant to explain.

"He'll tell you about it." She led the way down the beach.

"Come on, Jean. You've got to be kidding."

When she didn't respond, Neil tried again. "This is a joke?"

"It's not a joke." She shook her head. "At least I don't think so. But I don't understand it, so please let QL47 explain."

It was late by the time they got back to the spot where QL47 waited, his white clothing the only spot of light in the overcast, moonless night. "Good," he said. "You got the blankets."

He'd been busy while she was gone, having gathered a good-sized pile of tree branches and even whole trees, which he'd obviously pulled up by the roots. Jeanette looked at QL47 with a new respect for his strength, remembering what Neil and Jesse had said about the ironlike wood.

"What are those for?" Neil touched the pile with his foot. "If you're planning to make a fire, it won't work. The wood's too green. Besides I'm not sure that stuff would burn even if it was dry."

"No fire." QL47 shook his head abstractedly. He pointed to the heap of foodstuffs and containers of fluids. "You'll have to be conservative. Van collected a generous amount for one person, so it will be a scanty supply for three."

"QL47, you sound as though you're not going with us," Jeanette accused.

"Are we going somewhere?" Neil demanded.

Jesse didn't say anything. She looked doubtfully at the small stock of supplies.

QL47 reached into his pack and pulled out the little packet Van had given Jeanette. "Technological developments such as miniaturization are not known to the public in general, but as I've mentioned before, Van Lee was most resourceful."

"Van Lee *is*!" Jeanette insisted.

QL47 inclined his head slightly. "Ummm, yes, I suppose so. Nevertheless, he has left you a legacy that will be most useful. He did not come unprepared to prison island."

"You said that thing was a boat." Jeanette blurted out the accusation.

"Come on!" her brother said. "Nobody could ride on anything that tiny."

QL47 allowed himself the rare luxury of a smile. "We will see, won't we, Neil?"

He walked over to the water's edge and waded in to the ocean. "As I've been trying to explain, miniaturization is a most useful tool. It allows ease of storage and handling. What Van Lee has presented us with is an advanced example of the art, a means of transportation across water that is capable of carrying several people." He spoke like a teacher giving a lecture.

Jeanette and the boys followed him to the water's edge. In the darkness, it was difficult to see what was going on.

"I will now pull the tab," he went on as though delivering a step-by-step lecture, "dropping the packet into the water as I do so, but keeping hold of the tab as it pulls out."

They stood watching as he went through the actions he'd described, then jumped back hurriedly as an object suddenly ballooned up, growing so rapidly that in spite of himself, QL47 was knocked over into the water.

"QL47?" Jeanette called anxiously as Jesse rushed to help.

"I'm fine. I'm fine." He splashed through the water toward them to stand dripping on the sand, a long cord held in his hand. He gestured toward the thing that had grown in the water. "How's that for instant transportation?"

It was a large raft, almost invisible, the same blue green as the ocean water. QL47 held it by a thin strong cord, which he used to pull it toward them. "The current's tugging it out," he said. He turned to look at them, quite pleased with himself. "Don't just stand there with your mouths open. Get ready to go."

"QL47, how did that happen?"

"It is constructed of a newly developed fabric that has properties that allow it to be reduced, then stretched to many times its apparent size. Once the tab is pulled, the process is begun and a chemical reaction inside causes it to draw in air, gulping it in at an enormous rate. All I had to do was pull the tab and then seal off the opening when a sufficient quantity of air had entered. But, I must insist, we really don't have time to stand around talking. What if the protectors grew interested in what we find so fascinating about this end of the beach?"

Jeanette nodded numbly. "I guess we need to get the food on board."

"That and the tree limbs I gathered. With them you can construct a primitive shelter. It will guard you from the sun as well as providing a little privacy."

Jeanette and the boys hurried to obey. It wasn't until they had everything on the raft that what QL47 had said really penetrated. "Aren't you going with us?"

He shook his head. "I feel my duty is here with Van Lee."

"But you don't even like him! Besides, you know we'll come back for him."

"That's the reason I'm staying. You cannot afford the time required to come back. You have other things to do. But I . . . Well, I have at least two centuries before my power supply begins to diminish, and Van's condition is such that time is not essential to him either. It will take time, years perhaps, for me to find a way to undo what has been done to him. But I am patient."

Jesse stuck out his hand. "We'll miss you, QL47."

"And I will miss you." QL47 shook hands with formal dignity, then went immediately back to his role as stern instructor. "The currents will carry you, their rate of motion such that you should arrive on land in approximately three days. The sea is relatively unused these days, so your main danger will come from the air, but your raft will not be easily spotted."

"Won't the guardians coming looking for us?" Neil asked.

"I will contrive to keep your absence secret as long as possible by sending messages of confusion into the guardian network. Hopefully they will not even know you've gone until you've safely crossed the strip of sea that lies between here and the mainland."

"And when we get there?" Jesse asked the practical question.

"You will arrive on a rocky, uninhabited coast. Go north for ten and a half miles and you will find a transporter tube. It is open, clearly visible and not limited in use since it is in an area normally crossed only by guardians. Enter it. You will come out in the guardian city at a location close to the timeway."

"And then we'll have the protectors to deal with," Jesse added grimly.

"Not alone. I will send messages to confuse them. They will be drawn from the building, leaving you clear access, if my plan works."

"If?" Jeanette asked.

"I cannot be certain that I can still communicate over such a long distance. Another factor is timing. I have calculated how long it will take you to reach land and to walk to the transporter tube. I must assume that you will step out of that tube as the sun reaches the middle of the sky on the fourth day."

"The fourth day," Jesse nodded. "We'll do our best."

Everything they needed was on board. They said goodbye to QL47, finding words less than useless for the occasion, and climbed onto the raft.

QL47 pushed them out into the dark water, wading into the water up to his waist to do so, and soon they were caught up in the current, drifting rapidly away from the island.

Jeanette watched the glimmer of white that was QL47's clothing as long she could see it. "Now you'll have to admit that we can trust QL47, Jesse."

He smiled, his teeth a flash of white in the darkness. "I reckon you were right about that, Jeanette."

CHAPTER NINE

At the end of the third day, just as the setting sun was sending a rosy glow across the sea, they came to land: tired, hungry, and sunburned. Jeanette stepped up on to the rocky beach, feeling as though the waves still bounced under her feet.

"We made it," Neil said, sinking down at her side.

Jesse was last to come ashore, having gathered up their soggy blankets. "Nothing else on board that we'd want to keep. Not even a scrap of food."

"And I'm starved!" Neil announced.

"Guess we let this thing go?" Jesse asked, still holding on to the raft's cord. "Seems to me that's the thing to do in case they're already looking for us. We don't want them to know we landed here."

They nodded agreement and he released the cord. The raft, pounded by the water against the rocks, bounced along the shore, edging slightly southward. Jesse sat down beside them. "Quite a trip. That one time I thought the airplane would spot us for sure."

"But he didn't. We made it." Jeanette couldn't believe it. "And the unfair part is that you got tanned. Neil and I only turned red."

He grinned. "I'm used to working out in the open. My skin's already toughened up."

Jeanette touched her peeling nose, wishing she could have a bath, some sunburn cream, a huge meal, and then a good long sleep in a comfortable bed. Well, at least she could have part of that. She could find a protected spot on the beach and curl up for a long night's undisturbed rest on solid ground. "I don't know about you guys, but I'm going to find a nice place to spread my damp blanket. Anything will be better than rolling with the waves all night."

"Better not, Jeanette. We've got to get going."

"Going," she wailed. "Where?"

"QL47 said it was over ten miles to the transporter tube. And we're exhausted and not likely to make good time. We need to walk part of the way tonight. By doing that we'll be sure we can get there on time tomorrow."

"No! No!" He was right and she hated to admit it because she felt too miserable to take an unnecessary step. The terrain ahead looked rugged, full of rocks and low hills, with taller mountains in the distance.

"Ten miles isn't far."

"Ten and a half miles," Neil corrected, sounding as exhausted as she felt.

"Maybe it's not far to you," she told Jesse, "but Neil and I aren't conditioned to the rugged life."

"I could go on alone. You and Neil are worn out."

It was the one argument she couldn't deal with. "Okay, you win. We'll go."

"Not me." Neil stayed where he was, his head drooping and his shoulders sagging.

She propped her hands against her waist. "Neil Lacy, you'll just have to get up from there and come with us. How would I ever explain to Mom and Dad if I came home without you."

"They wouldn't care, not since they got the divorce. They're both too caught up in new lives to care about us."

"Oh . . . bosh! You know that's not true. You're only feeling sorry for yourself. Now come on."

It took every ounce of strength she had to keep Neil and herself going, but before they finally stopped to rest, Jesse told them proudly that they'd covered half the distance. "We're not making good time because we're so tired from that long raft trip, but tomorrow will be easy now."

It was another dark night and Jeanette had no choice but to settle into her blanket without even knowing what she might be sleeping on. She couldn't even see the countryside ahead and could only hope it wasn't populated with wild animals. The two boys made their beds on the opposite side of a big boulder, sharing the other blanket.

"At least the blankets dried while we were walking," Jeanette called.

Nobody answered. She wondered if they were already asleep. Tired as she was, she couldn't fall asleep that easily. She looked up into a scattering of stars, the sky behind them a mass of darkness. She sighed and turned over, trying to get comfortable. She hoped Jesse knew what he was talking about when he said they were going in the right direction. She couldn't see how he could possibly tell which direction was which, but he claimed to be able to judge. She supposed he'd had lots of experience finding his way across lonely lands.

She was almost asleep when a voice called from the other side of the boulder. "I'm so hungry."

"Go to sleep, Neil," she called. "We'll get something to eat tomorrow."

But now all she could think about was food. She thought of the big breakfast Jesse had made for them that morning at home: ham, eggs, pancakes. Her stomach felt hollow. She wouldn't even mind another meal of dehydrated fruit and concentrated juice. Her mouth was dry. They hadn't found any source of fresh water since they landed.

It took a long time for her to fall asleep. When she woke up, the sun shone brightly from high in the sky. She sat up abruptly, blinking at the landscape.

Now she could see what had been invisible

the night before. Just ahead of them lay barren, rocky mountains!

Mountains, and they'd overslept!

She couldn't believe she'd actually awakened before Jesse. No doubt he'd been exhausted too and all that talk last night about being used to the rugged life was just to keep them from giving up.

She jumped up, pushed her hair into place as best she could, and dusted off her well-worn yellow suit. If she ever got out of this, Jeanette decided, she would never wear yellow again. She peered around the boulder.

She almost hated to wake them up. Neil's face looked scalded, burned crimson from the sun that had shone down on them as they crossed the sea. Jesse had turned over on his stomach, his head pillowed on one arm. They both looked so tired.

"Jesse," she called softly. "Neil."

Neil moaned, rolled over, and went back to sleep. Jesse's body stiffened, then he sat up, instantly alert.

"It's all right, Jesse. It's only me."

He glanced at her, then at the sun. "We've overslept."

She nodded. "I'm afraid so. And we've got a rugged climb ahead." She pointed toward the mountains.

He stared as though he couldn't believe his eyes. "You would have thought QL47 might have mentioned a little detail like mountains in our way."

"They're not tall mountains."

Jesse laughed ruefully. "No, and to QL47, who doesn't get tired, they wouldn't seem like much of an obstacle. Well, Jeanette, you'd better freshen up while I get your brother on his feet. He can be slow to wake up."

Jeanette got the hint. Jesse was from a more discreet era. He was offering her a chance for privacy before the long walk ahead.

She'd strolled over a little rise and was thinking how thirsty and hungry she was when she heard his call. "Ready to march."

She wasn't ready, but didn't seem to have much choice. When she rejoined them she found them both sleepy-eyed and rumpled looking. Neil was trying to pat down hair that wanted to stick straight up in several places. "So thirsty." He sounded like his mouth was glued shut.

"We'll surely find water today." Jesse tried to sound cheerful.

Jeanette looked at the rocky slopes with almost no greenery that lay ahead. How could he be sure they would find anything to drink? But nothing was to be gained by saying aloud what they all knew. "No matter. We'll be to the transporter tube before we know it."

Jesse nodded and started off, Jeanette following, and Neil coming after her. Jeanette couldn't help but be conscious of how far overhead the sun was in the sky. How late was it? Did they still have time to reach the guardian city on QL47's schedule? She decided that, like the problem of water, this was something she might as well not worry about. It was better to spend what energy she had on moving ahead as rapidly as possible.

None of them said much as they scrambled up the foothills, following Jesse's lead. As Jeanette had pointed out, the mountains ahead were not exactly towering, hardly more than particularly tall hills, but most certainly their progress would be slowed.

By the time they were climbing in earnest, scrambling their way up stony slopes, Jeanette found she was unable to think of anything but the necessity to take the next step and crawl up the next boulder. Somewhere in the back of her mind, she was conscious that her body screamed for food and water, but that was like a dull ache she'd been living with for an eternity. She had no goal in life but to keep moving.

They climbed over the first mountain to find a deep valley between it and the next. "Sure to be water here," Jesse told them. "Looks like this valley was carved by a river."

He led the way downward and Jeanette was too tired to even think about the possibility of contaminated water. All she could think of was the feel of cool, wonderful-tasting water in her mouth.

"I think I hear water running over rocks," Neil called eagerly, running ahead of them.

"Can't be a very big river," Jesse said. "It looks like they've got real arid country hereabouts. Maybe it's only a stream."

"They say our branch of the Trinity used to be a giant river through our area," Jeanette said. "With terrible floods."

"That's the way I remember it," Jesse agreed. "It's sure different in your time."

"They did things to it, tamed it so it wouldn't flood. But where is it, Jesse, where's the river? It should still be here."

"Are you all right, Jeanette? We're a long way from the Trinity River, I reckon. This is another place and another time."

She knew she'd been speaking from a scorched, thirst-inspired nightmare, but Jesse's matter-of-fact voice penetrated that haze. She tried to smile. "I'm okay. Just hot and thirsty and wondering where this elusive river of yours is."

Her heart sank when she heard her brother's cry of disappointment. "It's only a dry bed. Sand! That's all there is, just dry sand."

They found the energy to run ahead and confirm his words. The riverbed didn't contain as much as a puddle of water.

"Water probably runs down from the mountains when there's lots of rain up there, but the rest of the year it's dry," Jesse told them. "I've seen places like that. Riverbed can be dry as this and suddenly a wall of water rushes down from the mountains, covering everything."

"I wish it would rush down now," Neil said.

Jeanette was too disappointed to say anything. "Guess we'd better get going again."

"Yep," Jesse agreed.

Neil didn't say anything, but he started walking. No one said anything about giving up, but they all glanced upward where the sun seemed to be drawing perilously close to the center of the sky.

The next mountain seemed to stretch forever, broad as it was high, and when they got to the top they found a plateau. Jeanette sank down on a boulder, feeling that the only thing she had to be grateful for was the fact that going down was bound to be easier than coming up had been.

She looked up. The sun was almost in the middle of the sky. It was hopeless. They'd just have to run the gamut of the protectors around the timeway without QL47's help and that was like walking into certain failure.

Nevertheless, she got up. "We don't have time to waste."

Neil, who had dropped at her side, struggled to get up. Jeanette stretched out a helping hand to give him an assist. "Where's Jesse?"

He pointed. "He went on ahead."

She looked to find him standing on the flat top of the mountain. He gestured excitedly to them. "Come on," he yelled. "Hurry! We don't have much time."

As if we didn't know that, Jeanette protested inwardly. Hurrying was not likely to do them much good now with the sun almost at zenith.

They ran anyway. When they reached his side, they found him smiling broadly, the fatigue banished from his face and his brown eyes sparkling. "It's here!"

Then she saw what had so elated him. There, built right in the mountain, was a transporter tube.

She stared in disbelief. "I didn't think we'd come that far."

"It seemed like forever." Even Neil sounded stronger, though his voice croaked from dust and thirst.

"Forever, but not far enough."

"I must've misjudged last night. We covered more ground than I thought."

"Well, let's go." Neil headed toward the transporter tube.

"Not yet. We've got to calculate as precisely as we can if we've got a hope QL47 can help us. Another minute yet." Jesse stared at the heavens.

Jeanette hadn't known a moment could seem so long. Somewhere in the distance she heard a stone tumble down the mountainside, crashing against the boulders in the valley floor below. What if QL47 couldn't help them? Even he hadn't been sure his communicative powers could still reach so far or that he could cause confusion among the protectors who guarded the timeway.

"Now!" Jesse said. He was the first into the transporter tube. Neil didn't hesitate to follow him. Jeanette found herself alone in that vast and silent land, then stepped into the tube.

She was deposited gently on the other end and stepped outside to find Jesse and Neil waiting for her. The gray buildings and landscape of the guardian city loomed depressingly around them.

They didn't stop to talk about it, but took off running, following the directions QL47 had given them to the timeway building. No guardian, no one at all, was visible on the streets. That could mean, Jeanette knew, that QL47's plan was working. But it could also mean the opposite. Perhaps the guardians knew already of their arrival and were clustered in the timeway building, waiting for them.

No time now to debate choices. Jesse's longer legs kept him just ahead of them, but energy had come from nowhere for both Jeanette and her brother and they were able to keep up.

Then Jeanette recognized the timeway building just ahead and looked up. The sun was in the middle of the sky.

"This is it," she heard Neil mutter, more to himself than anyone else.

Jeanette nodded agreement. Now was the moment when they found if it was all worthwhile: having to leave Van and QL47 behind, that terrible ocean crossing on a raft, and finally last night sleeping on the ground and then the climb this morning with all the misery it had cost.

Once again Jesse led the way and Jeanette didn't challenge his leadership, knowing it was pointless to do so. It didn't matter anyway. Whatever happened now would happen to all three of them. They were in this together.

They ran down long, deserted corridors of the timeway building. So far, at least, the plan was working. Normally protectors would be thick in this area, preventing entrance to the building.

Either it was working or they were all gathered by the timeway, waiting for them.

They kept running.

"Nobody there." Jesse's loud whisper drifted back to them. "It's worked."

They slowed their pace slightly and Jeanette drew abreast of Jesse to see that it was true. The timeway stood unguarded.

CHAPTER TEN

Jeanette couldn't believe her eyes. She kept expecting her old enemy, the captain of the protectors, to jump out at them. "We've got to hurry," she whispered, "before they begin to figure out whatever ruse QL47 has misled them with and come back for us."

"Where do we go now?" Jesse asked. "The future? The day when Amy's people landed?"

She nodded. "Keep it firmly in mind, Neil, because you haven't actually seen it before. The timeway is as deserted as it is now because everyone is outside. The aliens are landing in small spaceships that have transparent domes so they look like bubbles. And the protectors are shooting them down with rays of light that make them explode."

"But later," Jesse cautioned. "Late in the day

after we left. You remember we've been warned about running into ourselves."

"I'll be careful," Neil said, sounding a little annoyed with all their warnings. "I'm not a baby, you know."

They sent Neil, as youngest, on ahead. The last thing he said as he stepped onto the timeway steppingstones was, "I hope they have something good to eat and drink."

Jeanette laughed softly. She looked at Jesse. "You go next."

He looked at her uncertainly. "I'm not sure whether it's more dangerous to be first or last."

"Go ahead," she urged, still laughing. "You'll be waiting for me."

He jumped up on the stones, shimmered, and vanished. Jeanette hesitated a few seconds before following. She couldn't help thinking about the nature of time and how they could walk through it this way. Time, the mysterious barrier. Her mind seemed to be trying to make some new connection.

She heard a sound far in the distance and recognized it with a leap of her heart. The heavy feet of protectors running down the long corridors toward her!

She jumped on the stone and pictured firmly the time where she wanted to go: the future, 2099, and somewhere in that distant world Amy and her people were waiting.

She welcomed the swirl of colors that told her she was moving through time; the familiar rising sound sang in her ears. She'd never been so glad to leave anyplace as that repressive time of the guardians.

She wasn't even afraid of the dumb darkness and silence of the center: time itself was becoming a familiar medium. Moving through it no longer seemed so strange and threatening.

When she saw Jesse and Neil waiting for her, she was glad that she'd been the last to travel. It was good to see them there already. She stepped off the timeway into a building as empty as the one they'd entered a few minutes before. She hadn't been sure it would be this way. She hadn't been certain but that the protectors would be guarding it again.

"It's been a long way," Jesse said, his face pale, "but we finally made it back."

She nodded, breathing deeply as she tried to quiet her own climbing tension. "If only we're not too late. If only Amy . . ." She stopped because she couldn't allow herself to say the rest of it. Her friend had to be all right.

"We have to be careful going out of here," Jesse told them. "It was awful out there last time."

Jeanette looked sternly at her brother. "Warfare," she said succinctly, "between the protectors and the aliens. And if you get killed, Neil, we wouldn't be able to undo it. So be careful."

He looked annoyed. "Don't talk to me like I was a baby, Jean."

Vaguely she wondered if he still thought he was going to be the time keeper someday. She hoped not.

Jeanette wouldn't let Jesse take the lead this

time, but walked at his side, Neil trailing indignantly just behind them. The long corridors of the timeway seemed abandoned, but from outside drifted the horribly familiar sounds of that battle they'd visited once before.

When they approached the opening that led outside, they pressed themselves against the wall and crept carefully forward, trying to keep out of sight as much as possible.

"What is going on out there?" Neil whispered.

"We told you," Jeanette whispered back in annoyance.

"That was kind of a wild story, bubble ships and all."

"I didn't mean they were actually bubbles. They just looked like bubbles."

"Hush!" Jesse turned to look sternly at them. "This is not exactly a good time for an argument."

Jeanette nodded, wondering why she'd suddenly become so irritable. It was because she was scared! She couldn't help feeling especially responsible for her brother's presence here in this deadly place. Sometimes Neil could be so impulsive. He mustn't be injured.

"I'll sneak out first and see what's going on," Jesse whispered.

Jeanette had known him too long to debate the matter. She simply waited until he was outside, then glanced around at her brother. "Wait here, Neil." Then she followed Jesse outside.

Again they'd lost time in transmission. It was deep into the night, drawing near to the early hours of the morning. The bright flash of the protectors' weapons was like the dazzle of a fireworks display, the explosion of ships under attack like the sound of rockets.

She stepped close enough to Jesse so that their arms were touching and wondered what to do next. Everything they'd been through had been to bring them here. QL47 had said the aliens would all die without their intervention. And now they were here and the aliens were still dying, but what were they to do?

She felt someone bump into her from behind. "I told you to stay in there, Neil."

"And I told you to stay," Jesse whispered, not even sounding angry. She supposed he was getting used to her by now.

As before, the area around the timeway building was darkened, the center of action far down the street. "Maybe we should use the same tube we took before and try to find Amy," Jeanette whispered.

"That'd be best," Jesse agreed, inching forward.

Jeanette turned for one last look at the terrible scene being enacted before her eyes and gasped. A new element had entered the picture.

Something was approaching in the sky, a distant speck quickly growing closer. She grabbed Jesse's arm. "What's that?"

They stared upward as the lighted object seemed to zoom in above them. "Looks like an airplane," Jesse said, "but not exactly."

Whatever it was moved very rapidly, quickly drawing in to settle directly over the area of the worst fighting. "Looks more like a blimp," Neil observed practically, "but blimps don't move that fast."

"That one did," Jeanette contradicted, not taking her gaze away from the thing.

The protectors' weapons aimed fire at this latest intruder, but it withstood the light rays as though impervious to their power. Finally the attempts at attack slowed, then stopped, as though the protectors were trying to puzzle out what to do next. Their attacks against the aliens had been diverted and the constant swarm of little ships landed safely across the guardian city.

A strange silence settled across the area, broken only by the low hum of the tiny alien ships. Jeanette held her breath, sensing that something was about to happen.

Then a voice spoke as though from many speakers, sounding across the city, though it was directed from the blimplike airship.

"We are humans," the voice said. "Protectors do not battle humans. Guardians do not battle humans." The voice was calm, not unkind, that of a parent reprimanding a child.

The protectors' weapons were totally stilled.

Jeanette glanced at Jesse. "It's got to be some kind of trick. How can humans have built anything like that ship when they turned the world over to the guardians all those years ago?"

Jesse frowned, shaking his head. He didn't know either.

"Not only are we humans," the voice continued, "but so are those beings who are landing in the small ships all around you. By attacking and killing them, you are denying your programming. You are destroying those whom it is your purpose to protect."

"It's not so!" The cry came from more than one mechanical throat, full of anguish and doubt. "It's a trick to confuse us."

Jeanette recognized that voice. It was that of the protector captain who had so fiercely pursued them.

"It is so," the voice from the airship continued. "These who are landing on our planet now flee deadly peril on a sister world. They are our kind, not of alien blood, but our own cousins from across the stars. Far back in time we share a common heritage."

"From across the stars," Jeanette whispered. "Jesse, is he talking about your world?"

She sensed something like a tremor moving through the boy's body, then he stepped out from hiding into the light, stepped far enough away from them so that they were not included in his action. "It's true," he yelled. "We're people too. Why would you destroy us?"

Jeanette raced to his side and Neil wasn't far behind her. "We're people," she shouted, her voice hoarse with dust and thirst. "And you, the guardians, were meant to help us, not to control us."

A huge figure came barreling toward them. "Wrong! Wrong! They are wrong. They'll ruin everything." It was the captain of the protectors who shouted so furiously at them. "Seize them," he screamed to his troops, "before they can do any more damage."

"No," the voice from the airship thundered.

"You see before you Jeanette and Neil Lacy and Jesse Lansden. You should learn your own history. If you had, you would recognize those names. But you know enough to realize the truth when I say that one of them is keeper."

"Seize them! Seize them!" the captain screamed almost hysterically.

His troops didn't respond. Instead they stood, their faces wearing stunned expressions. A few moved about restlessly, but most stood still. The bubble ships were continuing to land and people in light-colored clothing began to emerge, their own faces betraying confusion and wonder.

Finally the captain raced toward the three of them himself, but when he would have grabbed them, one of his own men stepped between them. "No, Captain," he said firmly. "It is wrong to harm them. You are defective."

"Defective." The word echoed around them as it was repeated by protector after protector.

Jeanette drew a wobbly breath. "What's happened?" she whispered to Jesse. He shook his head.

"Beats me," Neil responded.

"We will now land," the voice from the airship announced. "Please meet us in the open square."

"Where's the open square?" Jeanette asked.

Jesse shrugged. "As your brother said, it beats me. But it looks like everybody's going there."

The now-docile protectors led the way with the aliens following more cautiously. Jeanette, Jesse, and Neil allowed themselves to merge with the crowd of newcomers. Within a few blocks, they came to a large open area where the airship already hovered.

As they watched, it settled into place on the ground. Immediately a hatch opened and several people exited. At first, Jeanette almost didn't recognize the tall person who led the way. She blinked. QL47? But he couldn't be here. They'd just left him behind on the island. He was still several inches taller than anyone who was not a protector and he was still dressed in gleaming white.

"QL47!" she cried, and began to push her way toward the crowd to reach him.

"Jeanette, Jesse, Neil," she heard him call. "Where are you?"

"We're here," Neil called. "But what I want to know is how did you get here?"

Suddenly they were all greeting each other and QL47 was laughing in a way that was entirely new to him. "You forget, I came through the normal process. It took me a little longer than you to get here, slightly over thirty-eight years in fact."

"Thirty-eight years!" Jeanette exclaimed, feeling almost faint with bewilderment. "But what do you mean? And, oh, QL47, what's happened? We failed and yet you're here and the fighting's stopped and people are acting for themselves again. What changed everything?"

His laughter this time was softer. He reached out to touch the tip of her nose in an affectionate gesture. "Your skin burned in the sun. I should have thought of that and found a way to prevent it."

His tone was gentle. It was like having Dad around to be worried about her again. "But you're wrong, Jeanette. The three of you didn't fail."

She was conscious that the whole growing crowd of guardians and humans were listening, trying to understand. She shook her head. "It doesn't make sense."

QL47 turned to gesture to the small group that had emerged from the airship with him. For the first time, Jeanette saw the slender girl with the long fair hair.

"Amy." She choked out the word in disbelief, then grabbed her friend. "You're alive. They didn't kill you."

"I'm okay. I'm fine. QL47 told us everything you've been trying to do to help us, but for me, Jeanette, it's been only a few, very scary hours since you left. And I've found my father."

A tall man, whom Jeanette had seen only once before from a distance as he placed the infant Amy on the timeway, stepped forward, smiling broadly. "It is good to meet my Amaleen's friend."

"Amaleen?" Jeanette looked at Amy. "Is that your name on . . . on . . ."

"On the other earth." Amy nodded agreement. "QL47 has told us that we are not truly alien but come from that other world where Jesse was born. But we come from centuries later, the other end of time."

"And you're alive," Jeanette said it again, hardly able to believe it. "You're safe."

"Your QL47 insisted on rescuing us. He knew of your fears."

QL47's expression turned grave. "The losses among the first wave were great, but now we have managed to bring it to an end. It took many years' work to get to this point, redeveloping the skills thought lost to those hidden away in the colonies, bringing humanity to life again."

"But how?" This time it was Jesse who spoke. "You said we had something to do with it, QL47, but that's not possible. All we did was leave the island and come here."

Instead of answering, QL47 turned to the man who stood at his side. "Don't you recognize me?" he stepped forward to ask. It was the voice that had spoken from the airship.

Jesse slowly shook his head. "Don't believe we've met."

"We heard you when you spoke from the ship," Jeanette said, "but I don't believe—"

He was a man who looked to be in his early thirties. He was small in stature, not particularly impressive in appearance. Already his hair was starting to thin on top. Something about his voice was beginning to seem vaguely familiar, though she couldn't place it. As though conscious of her confusion, he smiled, his eyes narrowing.

"Van?" She whispered the name, not believing it.

He laughed. "Thought you'd never recognize me."

It was more than she could take in. The long

hours without food and water, the hike across hills and the climb up mountains, had taken their toll. She felt herself beginning to sway and a darkness not unlike that in the middle of a time journey gathered around her.

As from a great distance, she heard her brother's voice. "I don't like to complain," he said, "but while you're all standing around here gabbing, we're dying of hunger and thirst."

Jeanette knew that she was tumbling to the ground with little dignity. It was not at all a graceful exit, she decided, before the blackness engulfed her.

The next thing she knew someone was poking a spoon in her mouth and saying, "Eat a little more broth, Jeanette."

Jeanette opened her eyes. The person with the spoon was Amy.

"The least somebody could have done," Jeanette announced, "is to have caught me when I fainted."

Amy grinned and it was like old times at school when they had been in class together. "You really mean Jesse, don't you? It sounds romantic and I think he's embarrassed that he didn't. He has this image of what a man's supposed to be like. But the truth is that he can barely stand up himself. Van is in there looking after him and Neil right now."

Jeanette looked around. She was in a tiny room, lying on a bunk. "Where is this?"

"We brought you on board Van's airship. We've even found fresh clothes for you, some lotion for that sunburn, and you can have a bath when you feel like it."

Jeanette allowed Amy to feed her several more spoons of the broth before trying to speak again. Already she was beginning to feel better.

"My people have suffered much this day," Amy told her. "But now Van has taken command of the guardians and they are out looking after the refugees. Their needs will be attended to."

"I still don't understand," Jeanette murmured.

"Nor do I. When you feel better, we will make them explain to us."

Jeanette managed to sit up. "I feel better already."

Amy frowned. "Somehow I doubt that."

"I've got to know, Amy."

After a minute, Amy nodded. "I feel the same way. Let's go find the others."

Jeanette's legs felt a little wobbly, but otherwise she didn't do too badly as they found their way through the ship to a small galley where Van and QL47 were seeing to it that Neil and Jesse didn't eat their soup or drink the tall glasses of fruit juice too rapidly.

"Slowly," QL47 was saying. "You don't want to be ill."

Van rose to his feet at the sight of the girls.

"Jeanette," Jesse croaked. "Are you all right?"

She smiled. "Wonder how long it will be before we even sound normal again. I feel as though I'd swallowed a lot of sand." She sat down, then looked up at Van. "Last time we saw you, you weren't doing too well."

His expression grew solemn. "I was never so

scared in my whole life as when they led me in for the webbing ceremony."

"Do you remember anything about it? I mean what it was like being in the web?"

He shook his head. "A total blank until the day when QL47 reversed the process."

"As I warned you, it took a long time," QL47 contributed. "Ten years before I'd regained the confidence of the guardians and several more before I'd come to understand enough about the process to safely reverse it. But as I told you, I'm a patient individual."

"I don't believe you said *individual* that other time, QL47."

He smiled. "It's the right word now, Jeanette."

Jeanette looked back at Van. "You were such a nasty little boy," she said.

He laughed.

"Van Lee is still a highly ambitious person," QL47 said. "Undoubtedly too much so for his own safety and comfort. But he is also a strong leader, something he would never have been if he hadn't met the three of you. Knowing you even those few days changed him. He became something more than a ruthless user of people."

Jeanette stared blankly, still not comprehending.

"That was it," QL47 spoke softly, "that was the intervention that changed everything. Meeting a young boy and producing a change in him that was to spread out to everything and everyone he touched. Van Lee is the leader of the movement that has stirred the people of this time back to life. And they are the ones who have saved the aliens."

"So that they didn't all die," Jesse said solemnly.

QL47 nodded.

CHAPTER ELEVEN

It felt good to wake up late the next morning, to feel clean and comfortably well fed, but best of all was just knowing that it was over! All they had to do now was go home.

Jeanette heard a stirring in the bunk bed opposite her own and looked over to where Amy was beginning to wake up. She still looked a little pale after the terrible day yesterday, but she managed to smile. "Your sunburn's faded a whole lot. That must be a great lotion that can heal so quickly."

Jeanette stretched lazily. "I feel much better." She got up and went in to the small closetlike bathroom to put on the well-worn blue cotton pants and striped pullover they'd given her last night. The clothing seemed comfortably familiar, much like the jeans and shirt she so often wore at home. She had no choice but to slip on the same shoes she'd had on before, but it was nice to be able to wear something other than the yellow coverall she'd had on for so long.

Amy giggled. "Those clothes are a little loose on you."

"I don't mind. It's great to know that there are some clothes around that weren't provided by the guardians."

Amy nodded. "What will happen to them now?"

Jeanette considered. "It seems to me that QL47 has provided the answer to that. He's shown that a guardian can be a friend and even think independently. I'd imagine that their role in society will be different from now on, but that they'll still be around."

Amy shivered slightly. "I'm still frightened of them, except for QL47, of course."

"That's natural enough. They've been the enemy for your whole life, though, of course, you can't remember back when you were a baby and your dad put you on the timeway to flee with Selma."

"Oh, but I do remember just a little now that I've been reminded. You forget, Jeanette, that my people have some special abilities."

Jeanette sat down on the bed. "I don't understand that. Everybody says we're really the same, just people, so how come you can do all those things that we can't?"

Amy shrugged. "We'll have to ask my father. He's highly intelligent," she added proudly.

Jeanette couldn't help smiling as she sat on the bed waiting for Amy to finish dressing. After all the years of having no family except Selma, Amy was really making the most of this. Selma! The very mention of Amy's longtime companion reminded her that many questions still remained to be answered. Before she died, Selma had said she was a member of an alien race and certainly the rocklike shape that had been her final state bore little resemblance to human form. The thought of Selma made Jeanette think of something else.

"You're in big trouble back at home. They've discovered that you've been playing hookey from school."

Amy came out of the bathroom, looking fresh and pretty in a soft pink dress that didn't fit any better than the outfit Jeanette was wearing. "Big deal. What are they going to do to me?"

"It's not so much that, Amy," Jeanette explained seriously. "They're worried about you. They'll probably be dragging the river next. And I only hope they don't arrest me for your murder."

Amy stared at her, then burst out laughing. "I can't go back there, but I will ask QL47 if he'll do something about the situation. I'd hate to think of you in jail."

"Me too," Jeanette assured her, relieved that the whole thing was to be turned over to QL47's capable hands.

In the galley, breakfast was nearly over, but Jesse got up to serve them cereal and fresh fruit. She smiled at him. "Now you can finally go home."

The smile faded from his face. "Sure," he said, "I can go home."

Frowning a little, she wondered what was wrong with him.

"I'm going to probably be in the black hole for missing so much school," Neil said glumly. "Might as well just stay here."

"What's the black hole?" Amy's distinguished-looking father asked with interest.

"In-school detention."

"You don't have to worry about that, Neil," Jesse told him. "Just go back five minutes after you left and you won't have missed anything."

"That's right." Neil's expression brightened.

"Only do be careful that you allow at least five minutes," QL47 warned gravely, "or you might run into yourself."

"What would happen then?" Jeanette asked.

QL47 shook his head. "We'd rather not find out. Those who have had such experiences have not returned to tell about them."

A cold chill ran up Jeanette's spine and she put down her spoon, suddenly not hungry anymore. She'd awakened this morning feeling that everything was resolved, but it wasn't, not by a whole lot!

"What about the timeway now that the protectors are no longer guarding it?" she asked. "Does that mean anyone who chooses can use it?"

QL47 didn't answer. He looked at Van and then at Jeanette. "What do you think?"

"Seems to me that if the three of us changed everything just by being there and acting like ourselves, it'd be too easy to make changes. Everything would be in constant motion and if somebody really tried to make things happen . . ."

Van nodded. "I've been there too, Jeanette, and I did a lot of damage. You're right, access to the timeway must be extremely limited. The guardians don't seem to have our curiosity, or our urge to experiment. They should still be the ones to guard the access into time."

"But we can use the timeways, can't we?" Neil asked.

Again Van looked at Jeanette. She didn't like the answer she would have to give. She shook her head. "We've got to go home, of course, but after that, I don't think so. It isn't a game. Every little jar, every accidental motion on the timeways, could set off reactions across time. We won't be able to walk in time again."

Jesse sat down abruptly, scowling at the table. Suddenly she knew what was wrong with him. She and Neil would go home and he would go home. They would be in different worlds, separated from each other by over a century of time. The thought made her ache.

And yet they had to go home.

"The steps are in our backyard now, QL47. Perhaps your protectors had better go there and remove them after we get home." She tried to smile. "I'm not sure I can resist that temptation."

"Besides, someone else might use them," Neil added regretfully.

"No." Van shook his head. "You three were keyed into the timeway when it was designed; the guardians all can use it, but no other humans except the 'aliens' of the later years." He smiled at Amy. "They were far in advance of us in their development of the uses of time, of course, and now perhaps they can teach us."

Jeanette wondered how she'd ever thought everything was answered. The world seemed full of questions. She asked the first one that came to mind. "But how did you do it, Van? You're not a guardian and you're not an alien. You walked in time."

He grinned, looking like the naughty boy she remembered. "I learned a little trick. You might say I hitchhiked."

"Hitchhiked!"

He nodded. "I stumbled onto a timeway near my home in Ontario at a time when the protectors were using it rather heavily. From seclusion, I watched until I was ready to make my own attempt. I learned that if I jumped on the second they left, then their coordinates worked for me."

"Is that what happened that first time for Neil and me? I've never been able to figure that out because now I know that logically we should have ended up in our own past, but instead we traveled across the stars to that other earth where unicorns are almost ordinary and a second moon shows up in the night sky."

To her surprise, Amy's father gave a strangled cry, a look of pain on his face.

"I'm sorry." She leaned apologetically toward him. "I'd forgotten it must be painful for you to talk about your home."

"That's . . . not it." He seemed to be having great difficulty speaking.

"Come, my friends." QL47 got so abruptly to his feet that Jeanette suspected he was deliberately changing the subject. "It's time to see you safely home."

It was like a party with everyone escorting them down the streets to the timeway building. Aliens and guardians mixed with Van's followers. A holiday spirit was in the air. Jeanette almost hated to leave.

At the timeway, Van made a speech, Amy kissed all three of them, even an embarrassed Neil, and QL47 positively beamed at them with pride. Neil was the first to be sent home.

"Be sure and remember," Jeanette called as he began to shimmer on the timeway, "five minutes after we left."

Jesse was next and that was the hard part. He didn't look at all happy to be going home. He said goodbye to everyone but avoided looking at her. She understood. It was the most painful thing in the world to think they might never see each other again.

When he stepped onto the timeway, she turned away so that he wouldn't see her cry, and when she turned back, he was gone. So quickly! She stared at the empty steps. "My turn," she said, her voice choked with tears.

"No, Jeanette," QL47 said gently. "Not yet."

Shocked, she looked around to find that he, Van, and Amy's father was regarding her with solemn, worried expressions. Amy looked as confused as Jeanette felt.

"For you, my friend, it isn't over yet," Van said, almost regretfully.

Knowledge that had been building gradually in her mind peaked to a certainty at the sound of his voice. He was sorry because he knew this was a responsibility she didn't want and would never have chosen for herself. "Not me," she said, her voice choked now with anger. "Neil's smart and Jesse's so special. It's one of them. It's got to be."

"No, Jeanette," QL47 said gently. "Each has a special destiny. Your brother's is particularly linked with mine, in fact, and Jesse will be the artist-photographer who preserves a fading time in pictures to be witnessed by the ages."

"But, of course, everything is still flexible, nothing is fixed," Jeanette reminded him of his own words. "Everything's still subject to change."

QL47 shook his head. "It has already begun. The path has opened."

Gentle-tempered Amy suddenly turned impatient. "What are you talking about?"

Jeanette didn't look at her friend. She was dry-eyed now, and when she spoke, her tone was harsh. "They're telling me that I'm the one, Amy. They're saying that I'm the time keeper."

It was as though no one dared speak while the moments moved past, but finally Amy's father came to stand at her side. "They have been waiting a long time, Jeanette. They have been waiting for you."

"They?" She stared at him in bewilderment.

"My people. The old ones, they who built the unicorn timeway."

She couldn't take it in. "Unicorns," she whispered, "because there were unicorns on your world and Jesse's."

He nodded. "Once we had unicorns. But now you must let me show the way."

They took her back to the airship and at a remarkable speed the ship flew them to a remote region of the planet. There they found the ancient ruin of a city where once-towering buildings were crumbling and sand blew down empty streets. Amy's father led them to an abandoned structure in the middle of the city. The air was stale inside, as though no freshness had moved through it for centuries. Near one wall in an inner room sat a figure from a long-ago carousel. It was the black unicorn.

"But what about the rest of the ride?" Amy asked. "What will make it go up and down? When we rode before, that's what happened. It started to rise in the air and then we were off into time."

Jeanette touched the still-glossy nose that reminded her of how it had felt to pet the soft nose of Lightning, Jesse's unicorn. "The unicorn isn't part of the keeper's timeway, is it?"

Amy's father shook his head. "This comes from our people and they're waiting for you."

Reluctantly, but feeling that she had no real choice, Jeanette climbed up on the unicorn, remembering that other time when she and Amy had ridden it to find themselves lost in the darkness, hearing distant voices.

The ride started off just like that other time. Colors shimmered, a rush of sound rose in her ears, and then there was only silence and darkness. The silence and darkness seemed to go on forever, and Jeanette knew she was moving across the centuries.

She began to hear the distant sound of voices. "She is not one of our own. She does not belong here."

It seemed impossible to speak from that numbed silence, but Jeanette managed to cry out, "I am the time keeper. I'm the one you've been waiting for."

Abruptly she was pulled from the darkness with a power that almost frightened her. Light, color, and sound resumed, and Jeanette's whirling senses came to a rest, and she found herself once more aware that she was sitting on a wooden unicorn.

"Welcome to the keeper," a gentle voice said.

The first thing her confused senses registered was that she was surrounded by people—very old people—with gentle, dignified beauty that extreme age sometimes brings. There were six of them, four women and two men, and they looked at her with kindness.

She swallowed hard. "I'm Jeanette Lacy," she said. "And this man back in two thousand ninety-nine told me you were expecting me."

She couldn't help feeling awkward and ordinary compared to the men and women around her.

They were dressed in wispy, graceful-looking clothing that reminded her a little of the way Amy's people had dressed. "This is the far future, isn't it?" she asked. Apparently the building she'd left awhile ago had totally crumbled; they were standing on barren desert sands.

"The fourth millennium is here. This is the beginning of the year three thousand."

Jeanette had suspected as much. When she'd heard the voices back in late December, they'd told her the fourth millennium was approaching. So now it was here! What did any of this have to do with her? It seemed almost rude to ask.

"You can ask anything you want, Jeanette," the woman who welcomed her said graciously. "That's why we're here."

Jeanette frowned. "Can you read my mind?"

"Not exactly, not unless you project your thoughts to us. We are used to communicating that way, you see. It started with the unicorns."

"Jesse and his unicorn did manage to get things across to each other in kind of an unusual way," she admitted.

The woman nodded. "That's where it began, why our world developed differently than yours. We took another path."

Jeanette thought of the aliens landing in the guardian city. "Did you take a wrong path?" she asked. "Is that why you had to escape?"

The six looked at each other, and she guessed they were doing some "communicating" that she couldn't hear. The woman turned to her again. "We did not take a wrong path, if by that you mean choosing an evil route. To us it seems that we went a better way, that our world was infinitely more beautiful, kinder, and wiser than yours."

Jeanette found that hard to believe. It seemed a little insulting. "Your people are seeking refuge," she pointed out. "Something must have gone wrong back in two thousand ninety-nine or you wouldn't have come here."

Suddenly she frowned. "This is still here? We are on my earth?"

The woman who had been appointed spokesperson for the group nodded. "It is your earth, Jeanette, but the refugees didn't land in two thousand ninety-nine. They started landing yesterday. It goes on today, tomorrow, and for the days after until all are brought safely to our new home."

Jeanette stared across the empty stretches of sand. "But I saw them."

"The tiny ships you saw would not have brought them across space. They came another way—through time, to us here. But in this first year of the fourth millennium the invaders have also reached your world."

"Invaders?" Jeanette stared at them.

"That's why we had to find the open door, the place where our people could go into your world without the invaders following. You provided it, Jeanette Lacy."

It seemed more of an honor than she deserved. "It wasn't just me. Besides, I think you should know that they don't all make it."

"We are aware that there will be losses. It is inevitable. But now those fleeing our world will find a place to belong, a world ready for them. We are sending them through time to two thousand ninety-nine. I am told that the population of that time had greatly declined. We think there will be room for new occupants."

Jeanette nodded. "I guess so. They don't seem to have many people."

The woman sighed, closing her eyes. "We have waited long, but now it is almost done."

"Almost?" Jeanette asked, more confused than ever.

"It is finished. Now it must be begun."

Jeanette decided this made absolutely no sense at all. Maybe these people were just plain whacky. "Who are these invaders?" she asked to change the subject.

"An ancient and dying race that has watched our people for a long time, waiting to take everything that was ours. We did not suspect, but thought the rose-colored moon had been there forever."

A picture flashed into Jeanette's mind. The second moon, shedding a hazy rose glow above Jesse's world. "But what was it?"

"It was the invaders, waiting out the centuries until their need was greatest and the time was ripe."

"They know about our world?" Jeanette's throat went dry.

The woman nodded. "But they do not move across time. They are an old and patient people, and they only step forward. They will not go back to endanger you and yours. And we," she gestured to include the little group, "we will remain here to do battle with them."

Jeanette couldn't help thinking that they seemed an awfully small force to do battle, but somehow she had a feeling they'd manage to do fairly well. "An ancient people," she repeated, then remembered. "That's what Selma said."

The woman smiled. "And how is Selma?"

"She died."

Jeanette could almost feel the ripple of sadness that moved through the group. "She was one of you?"

"Ah, no. She was one of them."

Jeanette moistened her lips. "The invaders?"

"It was the great thing that gave us all hope. No strain of life is totally evil for she whom you called Selma gave up herself to help the child, to help a whole race that was not her own."

"I see." Jeanette didn't see at all, but she decided she might as well be polite. "Selma was one of the enemy, but she decided to help Amy."

"She was the first of her kind to feel compassion for any member of our race. It happened because Amy's family was among the first to come here. We all knew that the early wave would stand the greatest risk."

The woman looked at her companions as though conferring, then nodded. "That was yesterday. Selma saw the child's mother lose her life and witnessed the helpless need of the infant. And now that we know they can care, we will know how to win over the invaders."

Jeanette nodded. "But why am I here? What does this have to do with me?"

It was as though the question put an end to all discussion. Once again, colors swirled and sound grew in intensity. Jeanette saw the faces of the old ones through a rainbow of sound and color. Nobody spoke, but she heard the words, "It must now begin." And then she was off in time again, heading toward centuries-long darkness.

This was not the keeper's timeway. She knew that now. Those six at the distant edge of time controlled it, managed even to intersect it with the timeways of her earth. "Let me see Jesse first," she called inside her mind. "It will be very dangerous; please let me see him first."

The motion seemed to slow as color and sound returned. The thought flashed through Jeanette's mind that she knew where it had started and that it involved Jesse. But she had to see him one more time before she risked her life.

As vividly as she possibly could, she envisioned him standing beside the timeway in his own world, waiting there for her. Then she began to come to a stop and could not longer feel the unicorn under her. Instead she was upright, standing on a stone step, and a tall figure was staring at her through the shimmering waves of color.

He advanced hesitantly toward her. "Jeanette?" he whispered in disbelief.

The person standing before her was no seventeen-year-old boy, but a man at least ten years older. She saw the dark eyes, the slim face, and had no doubt that in spite of it all, the person standing before her was Jesse Lansden.

"Jesse, is it you?"

He nodded. "But you look . . . the way I remembered. When I first met you . . ."

"I sent coordinates for you to be waiting here by the timeway."

"I didn't come back, not for years. I couldn't stand to because it hurt too much. I missed you something awful."

She reached out almost fearfully to touch his hand. "And I'll miss you."

His soft laughter rang through the cavern. "It's worth it, Jeanette. All the waiting. Because we will be together again. You just have to do it, discover the time principle, and it will happen."

"How can you be so sure?"

"Because I'm here now waiting for you . . . the grown woman. We're going to be together. We're going to be wed."

She smiled at the wistful, old-fashioned word. "Is it really true?"

He nodded. "We had time to cross, painful waiting to live through." He smiled. "But now we're going to have an inn, a hotel in a time between my world and hers . . . yours, Jeanette. A place where we can meet and be together."

She breathed the words. "The Lansden House."

She stepped backward toward the timeway. "I'd better go."

He nodded. "Before she comes. Before you run into yourself. That's dangerous." A familiar grin brightened his face. "Until later, Jeanette. Until the next time."

She stepped on the stone that would lead her into the future, then kept her eyes fixed on his face, seeing it shimmer and vanish, knowing that in reality she was the one vanishing.

Now the next step. She drew in a deep breath

and visualized the stones in the cavern again, but this time they were in her own world and three young people, a boy and two girls were approaching them.

It was a very dangerous thing to do, she knew. And yet it was what her mentors at the edge of time had said. She must begin everything all over again. It had surely started that day when she and Amy had followed Neil to the Lansden House basement to find him vanishing from the stone pathway.

She visualized the pathway, Neil vanishing, and she and Amy watching from the far end of the cavern in horror.

This had to be the answer. It was the only part that still didn't make sense. By everything she now logically knew, when first Neil and then she stepped on that stone, they should have gone into the past of their own world. But they hadn't, they'd ended up across the stars in the parallel universe where Jesse lived. That was where everything had begun.

Someone had to have been in the cavern giving coordinates that day. And that someone was Jeanette Lacy.

Surely, surely, it had worked and she'd survived. She'd just seen Jesse, and he'd told her they had a future together. That must mean she'd survived.

But QL47 had warned again and again that everything was subject to change. What had happened could be undone, the whole fabric unwoven until it was knitted again into a new design.

And, perhaps, she, Amy, Neil, and Jesse would have no part in that design.

Visualize! she ordered herself sternly. Think about the cavern the way it was that day. She tried to remember details. Neil had left his flashlight on the ground by the timeway. He'd stepped up first while she and Amy watched. She must be just a little ahead of them. She could hide at the edge of the cavern before they arrived. The picture in her mind changed, shifted slightly. Neil was just coming down the tunnel toward the cavern.

And then she was there on the timeway, in a panic to get off and to conceal herself at the dark edge outside the glow cast by the pathway. She heard footsteps. Neil! The light from his flashlight bounced from wall to wall, but didn't shine on her. Then he turned it off, put it down, and walked over to the timeway.

She felt fine so far, but had to remind herself that this was only Neil. She hadn't faced herself yet; the true test was still to come.

Neil stepped up on the timeway. Jeanette closed her eyes and pressed her hands to her temples, picturing the cavern in Jesse's world, the cavern to which they'd first journeyed. She heard a small cry and opened her eyes. Neil was vanishing from the timeway and the person who had followed him had made a shocked sound.

A wave of nausea swept through Jeanette as she faced herself. She looked straight into her own face. Funny, she'd always thought she was ugly, but she really wasn't that bad looking. Her hair was shorter. She'd grown some.

A rushing sound seemed to envelop her, and she knew that it was the pounding of her own blood careening through her body, hammering against her temples. The pain was more intense than any pain she'd ever experienced.

The girl now approaching the timeway seemed unaware that anything was wrong. She seemed just fine. She turned to talk to her friend.

Jeanette gritted her teeth as she tried to hang on. Why didn't the other Jeanette go ahead and get it over with? Why did she stand there talking? Didn't she know there was no time to lose?

It seemed to take forever as a raw sickness rose from Jeanette's stomach and spread into a burning fever in her throat. Then the dark-haired girl stepped onto the timeway.

Jeanette fought to hold an image, sending coordinates on that place where they'd gone the first time, Jesse's world and time. It was hard. She almost blacked out. She wondered what would happen to the girl already in transition if she failed now. What would happen to them both?

She hung on until the girl had vanished, and retained the image in her mind afterward, hoping it was long enough even as she slipped down onto the damp floor, sinking into unconsciousness.

She had no way of knowing how long she lay there unconscious, but when she awakened she could hear sounds of shouting outside. Then she realized she'd been lying there for days. The hotel was about to be destroyed and Jeanette and Neil would be returning.

Still feeling very weak, she dashed for the timeway and again sent mental coordinates. This time she pictured the four stones in her own backyard and a time only five . . . no six minutes after they left. She didn't want to come in on top of Neil.

Light, color, sound were replaced with darkness and deep quiet, then returned again. She felt strengthened, almost herself again, wondering why she wasn't starving, dried out with thirst after the long days in the cavern. Perhaps it was something like when Van lay dormant. Maybe her body had not been alive enough to have many needs.

Jeanette's senses returned, she hardly saw the colors or heard the sound; she was leaning forward slightly, waiting for the sight of home. There it was, the brightly lighted windows shining through the shimmering colors of the timeway.

"Come on," Neil shouted.

The back door was pushed open and Keli came toward them, her eyes enormous. "I saw," she said. "I saw a flash of yellow, mixed with other colors and . . . But what did I see?" She rubbed her eyes. "The light's not very good out here, is it? I can't be sure of what I thought I saw."

"That's right, Keli," Neil said cheerfully.

Jeanette felt sorry for her. She'd been standing there, her mouth open with surprise, as they vanished. And five or six minutes later, she'd seen them return. No wonder their stepsister was a trifle upset.

"Is Mr. Calloway still waiting to talk to us, Keli?" she asked.

"Mr. Calloway?" Keli asked, looking blank. "Oh, you mean the assistant principal from school. Oh, sure, he says he wants to reassure you again about Amy. But what happened to your clothes? You and Neil were wearing those red and yellow things . . . yellow!" She stared at Jeanette.

Jeanette ignored the question in her gaze. "Mr. Calloway wants to *reassure* me about Amy?"

"He thinks you were being a tiny bit hysterical to get so worried about her. But he says your loyalty is commendable and he wants to tell you again that the school authorities have received a letter from her father and he says she's fine and very happy at her new home."

Jeanette smiled. "That's good to hear," she said softly.

As they went into the house, she turned to glance back into the yard. The glowing stones were gone.